J ATINSKY
Atinsky, Steve.
Tyler on prime time / Steve
Atinsky.

Tyler on Prime Time

Steve Atinsky

Delacorte Press

Published by
Delacorte Press
an imprint of
Random House Children's Books
a division of Random House, Inc.
1540 Broadway
New York, New York 10036

Visit us on the Web! www.randomhouse.com/kids
Educators and librarians, for a variety of teaching tools, visit us at
www.randomhouse.com/teachers

Library of Congress Cataloging-in-Publication Data
    Atinsky, Steve.
    Tyler on prime time / Steve Atinsky.
        p. cm.
    Summary: While visiting his uncle, a writer on the most popular show
on television, twelve-year-old Tyler auditions for a part on the show.
    ISBN 0-385-72917-0
    [1. Television—Production and direction—Fiction.]   I. Title.
PZ7.A8575 Ty 2002
[fic]—dc21   2001032468

The text of this book is set in 11.5-point The Serif.
Book design by Melissa J Knight

Manufactured in the United States of America
April 2002
10   9   8   7   6   5   4   3   2   1
BVG

For my mom and sister

ACKNOWLEDGMENTS

My thanks to the following people for their advice and support: Aurora Roman, Kristin Burcham, Katie Zeiner, Bill Thomas, Lisa Fredrickson, Nancy Balbirer, David Warick, Amy DeBartolomeis, Margo Katz, Bill Idelscn, Ellen Plummer, Bill Habeeb, and Gail Parent. Special thanks to Joan Slattery, Jodi Kreitzman, and most of all, Beverly Horowitz.

Tyler
on
Prime Time

1

"**More** peanuts?"

She must have been the oldest flight attendant in the world, and she hovered over me with a look on her heavily made-up face that said, *Poor kid, traveling alone; maybe some extra peanuts will cheer him up.*

"No thanks," I said.

"We might have an extra chocolate chip cookie up in first class. They're warm."

"That's okay. I'm fine. Really."

"Well, just let me know if you need anything," she said, and moved down the aisle with perfect balance.

I appreciated the sympathy, but it really wasn't necessary. Why? Because I was on my way to Hollywood, soon to be a star. The way I saw it, one day, in the not-so-distant future, that veteran flight attendant would be sitting in some airport lounge talking about the good old days of aviation, when this face would come on the TV screen. He'd look familiar: a skinny twelve-year-old with sandy blond hair. Suddenly it would hit her that the boy she'd offered extra peanuts and a first-class cookie to was none other than Tyler Stewart, television star.

I was about to spend the next couple of weeks with my uncle Pete. Pete is a writer for the most popular show on television, *Kids in the House.* If you haven't

1

seen it, you've been living in China, or on a desert island, or your parents are public-television pledge drivers who only allow you two and a half hours of educational programming a week.

Kids in the House is a half-hour sitcom about a good-deed-doer couple who can't have kids of their own so they adopt strays from all over. These are kids that nobody else wants, like when you go to the pound and get all mushy for the ugly mutt with the broken leg and sad eyes who's pressed himself into the corner of his cage. Then you take him home and find out that he also does stuff like eat paint and turn your shag carpet into his own personal pee pond. You still love him, but you never know what kind of trouble he's going to get into next. That's sort of what it's like with these kids. People who write comedy, like my uncle Pete, call it *hijinks*.

The show's been on for half of forever, and every year some kids leave and some new ones come into the cast. I figured myself to be a natural for the show. First: I'm funny. Really. Not an obnoxious class clown who'd do anything for a laugh, but someone, as they say in the business, with great comedy skills. I can do imitations and come up with funny things to say at just the right time. All right, not too many people know how funny I am—yet—but I crack myself up on a regular basis. In my head I'm a scream. Second: My uncle's a writer on the show. He's the one who taught me my first joke. Here it is: Two flies are in the kitchen. Which one is the cowboy? . . . The one on the range. I know, it's a groaner, but hey, it was my first joke. Third: For the next two weeks,

I'm practically an orphan myself, on account of my dad being too busy to look after me while my mom is vacationing in Cancún, Mexico, with her new boyfriend, Raphael. Talk about groaners.

Don't get me wrong; both my parents give me plenty of quality time. The quality with my mom is usually worry. At any minute I expected the phone on the back of the seat in front of me to start ringing. *Just making sure you're okay, honey,* my mom would say, trying not to sound like the worrywart she is.

You should have seen her at the airport: "This is the first time he's ever traveled alone, so could you please keep an eye on him? He's been going through an asthma phase for the last few years, ever since the divorce," my mom said, giving more information than anyone needed to know, as always. "His inhaler is in his bag. It's the Chicago Cubs bag. Here's my cell phone number. If for some reason that doesn't work, I also wrote down my phone and pager numbers in Chicago as well as my e-mail address. I'll be arriving at the Sonoro Hotel in Cancún at about nine o'clock tonight. I wrote that number down, too." No wonder the oldest flight attendant in the world was trying to comfort me with peanuts and warm chocolate chip cookies from first class.

The main quality my dad offers is exasperation. He'll say stuff like: "I can't believe my kid got a C in math." Or: "Why do you want to waste your time playing computer games when it's a beautiful sunny day?" Or this one, which makes me want to cry or scream or both: He'll

3

knock on my head and say, "Hello, is anyone in there? Earth to Tyler. Earth to Tyler." I really hate that.

I was supposed to spend the last two weeks of August in performing arts camp, but the session was canceled. As I mentioned earlier, my dad (his name is Frank, by the way) told my mom (hers is Laura) that there was no way he could take me in. Big trip to Minneapolis. Big client. Big fight.

My uncle Pete had always told my mom that if she was in a pinch, he'd look after me. I don't think he ever expected my mom to exercise her pinch clause, since letting me out of her care is like getting one of the tigers at the Bronx Zoo to give up steak. Fortunately she has a new therapist who urged her to take this vacation. "The separation will be good for both you and Tyler" were Dr. Von Headshrinker's precise words.

It was all fine with me. In show business everyone needs a break, and this was going to be mine.

When the plane landed, I made my way toward the exit and tried to wave good-bye to my flight-attendant friend. No such luck. "Airline policy dictates that you must be accompanied by an attendant at all times," she said, and escorted me through that accordion-like tunnel into the terminal like I was a child.

When we entered the waiting area, Pete was nowhere to be seen. The two of us stood there while all the other passengers and crew deplaned.

"Isn't your uncle supposed to meet you?" my personal flight attendant asked, having been thoroughly briefed by my mom.

"He'll be here any minute," I said, then added, "He writes for TV," as if that would explain everything.

"Well, then, I'll wait here with you until he comes."

The two of us stood there looking at the steady stream of people walking through the terminal in our direction. Not one of them was Pete.

"You can go," I said. "I'll be fine."

Miss Friendly Skies of 1966 fell into that area reserved for school nurses and doting relatives: You couldn't avoid seeing them every once in a while, but the quicker you got out of their clutches, the better. "There he is now," I said, picking a man to wave at. "Uncle Pete!" I yelled, and started walking away from my chaperone into the steady stream of passersby.

"Have a nice trip," she called after me.

I ducked into a bathroom and waited for a couple of minutes. When I came out I was happy to see that she was gone. I took a seat by the arrival gate. An hour went by. It was now around six P.M. No Pete. No page over the loudspeaker for me to go to the nearest courtesy phone. I was starving. I wanted to go and buy a piece of lousy airport pizza but was afraid that as soon as I'd leave, Pete would come by, and then he'd start wandering around looking for me and so on and so on. I began to wish I had stocked up on peanuts.

Suddenly there was Pete, loping toward me, tall and thin, his wavy brown hair going in about twenty directions. He was still about fifteen feet from me when he went into his apology: "Sorry, Tyler. I forgot tonight was our first tape night of the new season and we had to do some rewrites and then I sort of lost track of time . . ." I should tell you that this is all typical Pete: losing track of time, wandering around saying he's sorry a billion times. ". . . and there was an accident on the 101 Freeway. I am really, really sorry. I have to get back. Are you hungry? There's food on the set. Let's get your suitcase."

We got the suitcase and tossed it into the trunk of Pete's blue Corolla. The guy makes a ton of money, and he still has the same lousy car he had when he worked in a video store. He also still rents.

"So, your mom and Raphael are in Mexico," Pete said as we pulled away from the white zone where he had illegally parked, resulting in the ticket that he shoved into a glove compartment that appeared to be filled with tickets.

As if I cared about stupid Raphael. "How's the show going?"

"Good. Good." He did a quick double take of me. "My God, you've grown! Are you shaving? 'Cause I'm all out of blades and if you have a few extra . . ."

"How can I be shaving? I'm twelve."

"You're twelve? That's too bad. I was going to ask you to drive." Going into a routine at the drop of a hat was also typical Pete. When I was younger he'd pretend not to recognize me at all:

You're not Tyler. I know Tyler. He's my nephew.

But I'm your nephew.

You are? You don't look anything like him.

We'd go on like that for twenty minutes. But not this time. Pete must have suddenly remembered that for the next two weeks he'd be temping as a responsible adult, because he stopped kidding around to say, "Tomorrow, first thing, we have to enroll you in day camp at the Y. Don't let me forget."

I knew it would never happen unless I reminded him about fifty times, which I was not about to do. Those things Pete didn't run late for, he often forgot entirely. On the day my parents got married, he forgot to put gas in their car, causing my dad to have to pull into a service station five minutes after having left the wedding reception. So I wasn't about to remind him to register me at the YMCA. I figured the more time I could spend at the studio, the better my chances were of getting a part on the show.

The conversation continued in an uncle/nephew vein: "You really have grown a lot, I'm not kidding. . . . So what grade are you going into? . . . Who's your favorite Cub?" That sort of thing.

Before long we were at the gate of the Universal lot. The guard waved to Pete, and we started driving past various soundstages and bungalows. Cool. After a while we pulled up to one of the soundstages and into a parking space that had Pete's name on it. Cool. Very cool. A banner hung from the front of the building. KIDS IN THE HOUSE popped in huge letters against an even huger picture of the cast. I took a moment to imagine my face right in the middle of the stars of the show. I then followed Pete through the soundstage door and into my future.

2

The first thing I heard was the roar of laughter.

When Pete ushered me into the studio, I expected to see the cast of *Kids in the House* on the set, up to their usual antics. It turned out that the laughter was for a stand-up comedian telling jokes at the front of the bleachers where the studio audience sat.

Soon we were right in front of the set. People were running around everywhere. Cameras were set up in front of the living room of Tom and Colby Parker, the do-gooder adoptive parents in the show. I felt privileged to be on the floor. People in the studio audience were looking at me, wondering who I was because you have to work on the show or be somebody's agent or relative to stand on that sacred concrete.

A large man dressed in jeans, a white T-shirt, a sports coat, and black tennis shoes came over to us.

"One of your friends from the playground, Pete?"

"Very funny. Tyler, this clown here is Neal Peachy. He's our punch-up guy."

I guess Neal could tell I didn't have any idea what Pete was talking about, because he said, "That means I get paid a ridiculous amount of money for working very little." A woman walked by; Neal was immediately on her heels: "Hey, Dorothy, wanna see my hyperlink?" And he was gone.

"He never turns off. Come on, let's get you something to eat," Pete said.

We walked behind the set. I figured we'd find the stars of the show backstage, but they were not among the people filling their plates from tables piled with everything from radishes to M&M's. The M&M's bowl was pulling my hand directly toward it. Pete stopped me in midgrasp: "Eat something healthy first," he said, plopping a huge hunk of lasagna onto a paper plate.

A girl's voice said, "That isn't healthy. Don't you know that cheese is like the worst thing you can put into your body except for maybe those M&M's?" The voice belonged to a girl in overalls with short, dark hair, green eyes, and freckles across the bridge of her nose. If you put a straw hat on her, you'd think she just fell off the bumpkin wagon.

"Exactly my point," Pete said. "Samantha, this is Tyler, my nephew."

"Hi," she said, and I hi'd her back.

We heard the stand-up guy say, "All right, let's meet the cast of *Kids in the House!*"

Food in hand, I walked with Pete and Samantha back to the front of the set. If you've never been to a live taping of a TV show, here's how it looks: The sets are laid out side by side. It's sort of like the set of a stage play but way wider. In this case, the center set was the Parkers' living room. There was a staircase that led to nowhere and a front door that did likewise. On one side of the living room was the Parkers' kitchen, and attached to that was one of the bedrooms. Several more bedrooms filled out the other side of the stage. There were also a couple of sets (the Parkers' patio and roof) out of sight or only partially seen by the studio audience, who could watch those scenes being taped by looking at one of the monitors above the bleachers.

"Samantha, can you hang out with Tyler for a while? I need to be with the other writers," Pete said.

"Sure," Samantha said. Pete then headed over to a small group of men and women, including Neal, who were huddled around a huge monitor split into four screens. Each screen showed a different picture of the set and had a letter taped to it: *A, B, C,* and *X.* Later I learned that the letters corresponded to each of the cameras that were now placed in front of the Parkers' living room.

The audience applauded each cast member as they were introduced. The first was the Parkers' Russian housekeeper, Sonya, played by veteran actress Josie Mayfair (you may remember her as one of the beauticians on *In the Chair*). Then came the kids, introduced youngest to oldest. I'm going to throw a lot of names at you, so I'll try to make this as easy as possible:

Razieh, age six, African American, played by Gary Wells.

Choon-Yei, age nine, Korean, played by Mia Hayes.

George, age nine, Native American, played by Steven Hall.

Grace, age thirteen, Caucasian, played by Gretchen Harris.

Marisol, age fifteen, Guatemalan, played by Faith Remo.

Devin, age seventeen, Caucasian, played by Eddie McNamara.

Finally the stand-up guy introduced Kari Franklin and Jerry Stone, who play the do-gooder adoptive parents, Colby and Tom Parker. The entire audience stood and cheered loudly when the stars came out.

Soon they'd be cheering for me, too, I thought.

Samantha, it turned out, was Kari Franklin's daughter. She was about half a foot taller than me, but I figured we were about the same age. In fact she was *exactly* my age. Same year, same month, same day (October 26). When you find out something like that, it's hard not to become instant friends.

The episode that night had to do with everyone in the house catching poison oak. It all started with George going down by a creek with a pal of his when they were supposed to be playing in the yard. When he comes home, he wrestles with Choon-Yei, who hugs her mom, who gives Razieh a bath, who plays alley-oop with Devin, and so on and so on until everyone in the house is covered in calamine lotion and scratching themselves into oblivion.

The audience was pretty much howling throughout. They laughed even harder on the second and third takes of a particular scene. Sometimes, however, if there wasn't a whole lot of howling going on, the writers would gather together and try to come up with a funnier line. This is where a guy like Neal Peachy comes in handy.

In between scenes Samantha introduced me to some of the kids on the show. Samantha was totally relaxed with these kid stars, probably because her mom was an actress and she was used to being around celebrities. I, on the other hand, had no idea what to say to them. Would other kids feel all tongue-tied and goofy around me after I became a celebrity, too?

Once, at recess, I had squeezed through a gate to chase down an errant volleyball and then couldn't get back into the schoolyard. I had to go all the way around to the front of the school to get back in, only to be greeted by the principal, Mr. Dykes. Another time, while on a field trip to the Chicago Institute of Art, I'd wandered off to use the bathroom (with permission), and by the time I'd found our class again, they'd been sitting in the school bus for almost twenty minutes waiting for me. There was an open house last year where I overheard my teacher, Ms. Kubalavski, say to my mom, "Tyler really is one of my best-behaved students. It's just that, well, sometimes—"

"He seems to fall into a pit of mischief?" my mom interrupted.

"Exactly."

A pit of mischief? I immediately pictured myself like some dopey and thirsty prehistoric beast wandering into the La Brea Tar Pits, to be forever enshrined in black goo. By the way, Pete told me if you translate the Spanish and say "the La Brea Tar Pits," what you're really saying is "The The Tar Tar Pits." Anyway, I sort of stumbled into the pit a couple of times that first night on the set of *Kids in the House*.

When they film a show, the cameramen sit with

their cameras on these carts, called dollies. They have people who move the dollies and still more people whose job is moving all the cables that are attached to the cameras. I must have been daydreaming about when I'd be on the show, because suddenly my feet got tangled in the cables, and the next thing I knew I had plowed right into Jerry Stone, who snapped, "What's this child doing here?" He didn't wait for an answer. Samantha came up to me. "You gotta be kind of careful around Jerry Stone. He's moody. My mom says he's irritable because he's in recovery."

"From what?"

"A failed movie career."

The other time that night that got me into the pit was a little more embarrassing. When they get ready to shoot a scene and want everyone to be quiet, they ring a bell, just like in school. The guy with the slate board had just announced the scene when the cell phone my mom had given me for emergencies (real and imagined) went off. All eyes were looking in my direction, searching for the source of the disturbance. I quickly answered. "Mom, I can't talk now. I'll call you later."

"You sound worried, honey. Is something wrong?"

"Mom, I really can't talk."

"But, honey—"

"Bye." I turned off the phone. Jerry Stone was staring right at me. "Are you through, kid? Because the people in the audience who came all the way from Yakima wouldn't want you to rush your call." I nodded while the audience laughed. Great, I've already managed to get in

Jerry Stone's hair. Twice. But then, when Pete collected me and escorted me into the bleachers, a funny thing happened: The audience clapped for me as I took my seat among them. Not bad, I thought. My first night in town and I get applause.

By the time we got to Pete's apartment, it was one in the morning. I'd been up since seven, Chicago time, but I was still wide awake. My mom would have said it was from the half dozen Cokes I'd guzzled down during the taping. Maybe. But I think it was because of how exciting it was to be on the set of a real live TV show, with real cameras (that really almost ran over me) and real stars.

There were about five messages from my mom waiting on Pete's voice mail telling me to call her in Cancún no matter how late we got in. So I called.

"Hello," a sleepy male voice with an Italian accent said. It was Raphael.

"Can I talk to my mom?"

"Yeah, Tyler, sure, sure, hold on." The direction of Raphael's voice shifted as he said, "Laura, it's your boy." Have I mentioned I hate Raphael?

My mom's voice came on the line: "Honey, are you okay?"

"I'm fine," I said. I had been excited to tell her about my first night in Hollywood, but knowing Raphael was right next to her suddenly made me want to get off the phone as quickly as possible. "I'm really tired," I said. "I just wanted to let you know I'm okay."

"All right, you get some sleep and don't forget to take your asthma medication."

"I will, Mom."

"And don't let Pete forget to enroll you in day camp at the YMCA tomorrow. Is he there? Let me talk to him. You get some rest, honey."

" 'Night."

Pete took the phone and got the reminder that I was pretty sure he'd forget by the time morning arrived. He then turned his futon couch into a futon bed and tossed sheets, blankets, and towels my way. "Sleep well" was all he said, and then he disappeared into his bedroom.

I started poking around Pete's place. Like I said before, Pete had been writing for TV for a few years now but this was the same apartment he lived in when he was working at a video store and doing stand-up at night. Same ugly green carpet, same cottage-cheese ceiling, same movie posters peeling off the walls. The only new things in the apartment were a flat-screen TV and a leather chair. I knew Pete did everything out of that chair: watched his new TV, read his books and magazines, ate. There weren't the usual crumbs all over the floor by the chair, so he must be springing for a housekeeper, too. It was a good thing, because the last time I'd been there with my mom, I had an asthma attack that was so bad that I had to be rushed to the hospital.

Then there was Pete's office, where he did everything he couldn't do in his chair. There were scripts everywhere. I mean *everywhere:* on his desk, on the floor, in his bookcase, on the chairs, and spilling out of the wastebasket. Then there were the books: dictionaries, a thesaurus, and massive New York Public Library reference books as big as telephone directories. There were books on how to write, how to sell what you write, and how to punctuate what you write. There was a cork bulletin board filled with photos, schedules, and little reminder notes. Not only were there the typical "to do" notes like "pick up dry cleaning," "get car tuned up," and "enroll Tyler in day camp at Y"—which I was tempted to toss into the overflowing wastebasket—but there was also stuff like "rethink career" and "find a mate" and completely silly notes along the lines of "renew lease on life" and "pay the piper."

I got on to Pete's computer and e-mailed my best friend, Frog. Some kids know everything there is about baseball players or computer games, or even cars, but Frog was the reigning showbiz king of Adlai Stevenson Elementary School. He was a walking *Entertainment Tonight*. I told him all about the show and the stand-up and Neal Peachy and Jerry Stone's wisecrack that scored me my first round of applause. Any info he could supply me on Jerry might be helpful, because I knew if I was going to get on the show it would have to be with his approval. I hadn't exactly gotten off to an approving start with the guy.

Even after all the food I'd eaten off the craft service table, I was still hungry, so I headed for the kitchen. On the refrigerator were Polaroid pictures of Pete with various actors and actresses who had done guest appearances on *Kids in the House.* Also, lots of photos with the cast of the show, many of the kids no longer in the house. I opened the refrigerator. Except for the cartons of leftover takeout and a few condiments, it was a beverage-only refrigerator. But nestled in among the beer, milk, orange juice, Diet Cokes, white wine, ice tea, berry juices, cherry colas, and various other liquids stood a gold statue. Pete's Emmy.

"How come you keep your Emmy in the refrigerator?" I asked Pete as we chomped on our Cocoa Puffs the next morning. Pete had won an Emmy for an episode of *Kids* that he had written the year before.

"It's in the refrigerator? I've been looking everywhere for that thing."

"Really?"

"I'm kidding. I keep it there, I don't know, so I don't take myself too seriously, I guess. And so I remember that if I don't write, I don't eat. Plus, I hear the things taste surprisingly good. They're chocolate underneath, you know."

It was already about ninety degrees outside by the time we got into the Corolla and headed over to the studio. A couple of things ran through my mind: One, don't say anything to Pete about day camp. He'll just naturally forget. And two, when would be the best time to subtly ask him about getting a part on the show?

"Um, are there any new kids coming onto the show this year?" I subtly inquired.

"Well, Grace's birth mother is going to show up on the Parkers' doorstep during November sweeps. They'll rebond and have a great old time. The mom will want Grace back, which will prompt the rest of the kids to secretly hire a klutzy private detective to investigate the birth mom's past. In the end Tom and Colby will let Grace decide for herself who she wants to be with."

"And she'll choose the birth mom?" I asked careful to mask my eagerness.

"Yep. Holy cow, we're gonna be late!" Pete said as he began to snake the car through traffic.

Great! I thought. *One of the kids is leaving* the House.

Since *Kids in the House* taped on Tuesday nights, Wednesday morning was when they'd have the table-read for the next episode. This meant that a bunch of tables were set up on the soundstage and the actors read the new script while the writers, designers, and network and studio executives all sat around taking notes.

I was happy to see that Samantha was there, too. The first thing she did was introduce me to her mom, who I'd somehow missed the night before.

Kari Franklin didn't bear that much of a resemblance to her daughter, except for her green eyes. Her face was rounder than Samantha's, and her red hair was covered by a brightly colored scarf. Even though she was dressed in jeans and a plain green blouse, she seemed to have an energy and presence that made you know she was a star.

Kari Franklin was America's favorite mom and, at the same time, Samantha's real mom, which must have been weird for Samantha. It hadn't taken me long to realize that Jerry Stone didn't seem to have much in common with his TV character, Tom Parker. It was different with Kari Franklin; yes, I knew she wasn't Colby Parker, but I liked her instantly, and she seemed like a regular person, even more so than some of the kid stars I'd met the night before.

"Sam tells me you were born on the same day," she said cheerfully.

"Yeah, quite a coincidence," I said.

"Maybe, if you believe in coincidences. I don't. I think the two of you were meant to meet."

"Mom, could you spare us the New Age hyperbole?"

"Such language from a twelve-year-old!" Kari gasped in mock shock.

Someone called out that it was time to start. Kari took a seat at the table next to Jerry Stone; Samantha and I sat in chairs that had been set up near the table.

"What's hyperbole?" I asked her.

"It's a fancy way of saying bull. What are you doing later?"

"Pete's supposed to register me in day camp, but I'm hoping he'll forget."

"Why?"

"I want to hang out here."

"Well, after they do the table-read, there's not a lot going on. The actors all go home and the writers work on the script. Wanna come over to my place?"

"Sure."

The writer at the head of the table, who appeared to be running things, was named Baxter Rhodes. I later learned that he was, in fact, what they call in TV the showrunner. I like job titles that tell you exactly what a person does. Most of the titles in TV are very misleading.

For example, Pete's official title on the show wasn't writer but supervising producer, but he didn't supervise anyone or produce anything except what he wrote. And how about grips—it sounds like a gang or something, but they were the guys who moved scenery, furniture, cameras, and anything else that needed moving. They should just be called movers, right?

Baxter had the look of a man who had, until recently, always been twenty pounds overweight. He wore glasses with round gold frames, and his cheeks had a pinkish glow. He introduced the guest stars and the director of this week's episode, who then read from the script. "Act One, the Parkers' living room, night."

The episode they read that day was the Halloween episode. It had something to do with the older kids not wanting to take the younger ones trick-or-treating. Other than that, it was pretty confusing, and nobody seemed to be laughing much except for a few of the writers, whose laughs seemed a little too large for the jokes they were laughing at.

Jerry Stone looked particularly unhappy. He was in close quarters with Baxter Rhodes, and words like "worst" and phrases like "where's the funny" wafted my way.

"We're in for a late night," Pete said as everyone dispersed. "Let's get you enrolled at that Y."

"Samantha says I can go over to her place."

"Oh, all right. I suppose we can wait another day. But how are you going to get back here?"

"Can't you pick him up later?" Samantha chimed in.

"I guess. When we take our dinner break."

"Great." Samantha then grabbed Pete's script, wrote down directions to her house on the back, and handed it back to him.

"Okay," Pete said. "I'll be by to pick you up around seven." He then handed me two twenty-dollar bills. "Here, this is for lunch."

"Where do you think we're going, the Four Seasons?" Samantha said. "We can eat at my house."

I handed Pete back the twenties.

"All right, I'll see you tonight." One of those "act like an adult" looks came over Pete's face as he turned to Sam. "This is okay with your mom, right?"

"Is what okay with me?" Kari Franklin asked, walking into our little circle.

"Tyler's going to come over to our house."

"Hi, Pete."

"Hi. Sorry about the script. I mean, we'll fix it."

"I know. You always do."

There was an awkward silence, which Samantha broke. "Let's go."

"I'll come by around seven," Pete said, waving his script and pointing to where Sam had written down the directions to their house.

"Your uncle's kind of a dweeb," Samantha remarked as he walked away.

"Sam," Kari weakly reprimanded her.

"Well, he is, and I think he has a crush on you."

"He does not."

"All the writers have crushes on you. Except for that guy Tim, who has a crush on Bruno in makeup."

"Samantha, you're embarrassing Tyler," Kari said as we walked out into the intense summer heat.

"Are you embarrassed?" Sam asked.

"No," I lied. The truth was that Sam's frankness did make me a little uncomfortable, but at the same time I liked it.

Sam and I squeezed into the passenger seat of Kari's magenta Jaguar convertible with a tan top. I couldn't believe my good luck. My second day in town and I was winding my way up the Hollywood Hills with a real TV star and her daughter. In a Jag!

Kari's house was way up in the Hollywood Hills. We had a clear view of the HOLLYWOOD sign as we pulled into the gated driveway.

Kari found me a pair of swimming trunks, and soon I was in the pool with Sam: splashing, diving, racing—you know, stuff you do in a pool.

Then we started to talk. I found out her dad was also an actor but had never made it big like her mom and had remarried and started a new family. Sam saw him maybe once or twice a year. He lived in Texas, which is where he was originally from, and taught acting and directing at the University of Texas in Austin.

"My dad's a lawyer," I said as we took turns doing chin-ups on the diving board. "He does a lot of work for Internet companies. For my last birthday, he had one of his clients design a Web site for me. It's called Tylertown.com, if you want to check it out later."

"Awesome."

"When I visit him, he almost always has a new girlfriend."

"Gross," Sam said sharply.

I looked up to see Kari bringing out a tray of sandwiches and potato chips. She set it down on the patio table, threw us a "You kids enjoy," and went back into the house.

We got out of the pool and started eating. "Wow, your mom is so cool. She's a big star and still makes sandwiches."

"You're so lame. Petra made the sandwiches. She's our housekeeper. My mom cooks, like, once a year—at Thanksgiving, where she has a nervous breakdown and swears that she's never doing it again."

We jumped back in the pool, ignoring the normal "half hour after eating" rule. After more splashing and diving, Sam got a couple of Cokes and poured them into glasses that had tiny umbrellas. We put on our sunglasses and stretched out on rubber rafts.

"Have you ever been on the show?" I asked.

"*Kids in the House?*"

"Yeah."

"No."

"How come?"

"I don't know. Don't want to, I guess."

"Are you nuts or something? 'Cause I'd do almost anything to get on the show."

"You and about a million other kids."

I wanted to say, *Yeah, but a million other kids aren't lying on a rubber raft in a pool, wearing shades, and drinking out of glasses with umbrellas with the daughter of Kari Franklin. And with an uncle who—at this very moment—is writing the words that will be heard by those million kids and their parents each and every Thursday night.* Instead I said, "I heard that Gretchen is leaving the show."

"Good. I hate her," Sam said.

"How come?"

"She's a pain. Her mom's a pain. Her agent's a pain. Her publicist is a pain. Everyone must have gotten sick of all that pain and written her out of the show. Happens all the time."

"Really?"

"Really. People get written out. They get fired. *A lot* of people get fired. Someone doing a guest part can be in the show on Tuesday, and by Wednesday they've been fired and replaced, and by Thursday that person's been fired and replaced too."

"Wow."

"And it's not just the actors. It happens to the writers, too. Ask Pete."

No wonder he was hanging on to his Corolla.

Kari's living room was as big as Pete's entire apartment. She'd fallen asleep in a big brown leather chair, a movie script in her lap, while Sam and I played Super Grand Prix Racing. I had just crashed my car for the billionth time—scattering a field of cows—when I told Sam about finding Pete's Emmy in the refrigerator.

"I told you, your uncle's a dweeb. But at least he's *got* an Emmy." She continued in an British accent: "Mummy over there says it doesn't matter that she's never won one; *'It's the work that counts.'* " And then back to normal: "But every time she loses, she goes to a spa for a weekend."

We played in silence for a while—if you don't count the sound effects of roaring engines, screeching tires, and screaming pedestrians—and then Sam asked, "Do you really want to get on the show?"

"Yeah," I said.

"Okay," she said. "Let's put together a plan. First thing we do: make some popcorn."

Sam put the popcorn into the microwave. "Well, it's a lot harder than it looks," she said. "Even with Pete's help you still have to get by the casting director, the executive producers, and Jerry Stone, who hates everybody. What kind of experience do you have?" I told her about some of the routines I did that always put Frog in stitches, including my "crazy legs" routine—that's when my legs have a mind of their own and I can't control them—and my imitation of a lobster being boiled. Sam didn't seem impressed. "Have you ever had an acting class?" she asked.

"Well, I was supposed to take one this summer but it got canceled."

"You should definitely try to get into one."

"But I'm only here for two weeks."

By now the corn was popping. "It doesn't matter. A couple of classes will help a lot, and you don't have to worry about getting in. The people who teach these things are usually desperate for money. I'll get you the name of one. In the meantime, start working on your uncle. It may be harder to get him to say something on your behalf than you think. People can be weird about this stuff. Okay?"

"Okay." And the microwave went *ding*.

7

Pe**te** picked me up at seven, remarkably on time. "That's 'cause he wants to impress my mom," Sam said when I told her of Pete's usual late act. "He's probably been thinking about coming here all afternoon." I was beginning to see what she was talking about. Pete wrapped himself around Kari's every word as she gave him a tour of the house, and even at a distance I could tell he was saying stuff that made Kari laugh. Pete knew his strengths.

"First thing we do tomorrow is enroll you at the Y," Pete said as I got in the car.

We pulled out of Kari's driveway and got a good look at the Hollywood reservoir as the sky was turning from light to dark.

"Can I go to acting class instead?"

"You want to go to acting class?" Pete had a way of repeating things when he wasn't sure how to respond.

"Yeah. Sam said I could learn a lot in a short amount of time." And then I added, so Pete wouldn't think I was a complete amateur, "to complement my natural talents."

"Hum, your mom really wanted to make sure you were in that day camp, and those acting classes are only a few hours at most."

"I don't mind hanging around the studio. Sam will

be there most of the time. And there's the Universal Studios Theme Park and CityWalk. And I could watch rehearsals."

"I'll tell you what, if it's okay with your mom then it's okay with me."

When we got back to the production office, there was a table set up outside the writers' room covered with picked-over pizza boxes and salad containers from California Pizza Kitchen. Pete and I loaded up our plates and walked into "the room." That's what the writers called it. The room. It was always: "Let's go back to the room," or a compliment for a writer might be: "He (or she) is really good in the room," meaning they contributed a lot when all the writers were gathered together. See, contrary to what you see in the credits, "written by So-and-so," most of the writing for most sitcoms is done in a group with the showrunner deciding what goes in the script and what doesn't.

Here's how it worked: First, the writers would come up with an idea for the story. Like, Grace finds her birth mom on the Internet. That would be the A, or main story. Then there might be a story of slightly less importance, say Marisol goes on her first date, and that's the B story. Add to that a third or C story, which is usually something just for laughs. For instance, the littlest kids go camping in the backyard.

Next, the writers break the story. On a big chalkboard they write down what happens, scene by scene. If the showrunner is happy with that, then one of the writers will go off and write an outline or synopsis of the episode. And if the network, Jerry Stone, and anyone else who has an opinion that counts okay it, then that same writer (or pair of writers) takes a couple of weeks to write the script. They then get notes from the showrunner, do a rewrite, and bring it back into the room, where the script gets a going-over from the entire writing staff. Sometimes the whole script will be rewritten. Who knew that a half-hour sitcom could be so complicated?

Next would be the table-read, which had happened earlier that day. Now the writers were in the middle of a page-one rewrite, meaning that there were lots of problems: not enough laughs, the stories didn't make sense, or Jerry Stone just didn't like something and said change it. So the writers had to go from the top of the script and rewrite the thing scene by scene.

They were all sitting around a large table as we entered. At one end of the room was a big TV. A page of dialogue was on the screen. I figured that was the script they were working on. Pete introduced me to the writers I hadn't met the night before. There were ten of them in all: seven men and three women. What I really wanted was to hang out in the writers' room, but Pete said I should wait in his office, which was right next door.

"It gets a little rough in there sometimes," he said.

"It does?" I pictured the writers getting into wrestling matches over whose jokes would go into the script.

"The language," Pete continued. "I don't think your mom would like it. That reminds me, you need to give her a call." He could see I was disappointed, so added, "Maybe another time. Look pal, we could be here pretty late. There's a TV in my office and a couch if you want to go to sleep. Oh, and you can use the computer if you want."

I went into Pete's office. It looked a lot like the one he kept at home. More Polaroids of Pete with various stars, lots of schedules and phone lists and scripts everywhere. He also had a dartboard—which I planned to make good use of—and various pieces of sporting equipment, including several footballs (one for indoors, one for outdoors), a couple of baseball gloves, a softball, a basketball, and a putter.

I dialed my mom's hotel in Mexico and was relieved when she and not Raphael answered the phone. She seemed relaxed for once in her life. She had just had a massage and lain down to take a nap. Raphael was by the pool. This was a perfect time to ask her about skipping day camp and going to acting class and spending time at the studio instead. Asking my mom for something was a lot like cooking: If prepared properly, everything came out great. First, I made sure she knew I was taking my asthma medicine (popping a pill in my mouth and downing it with a Coke as we spoke). Next, I told her about everything that had happened the night before and my day with Sam and Kari. I threw in some stuff about how safe it was on the studio lot. Security people everywhere. I then asked about her. Was she having a good time on her vacation? Seen any ruins yet? I didn't go as far as asking about Raphael. She would have

33

known I was up to something if I'd done that. Finally, after having properly buttered her up, I asked, "Hey, Mom, would it be cool with you if I don't go to day camp?"

"I don't know, honey . . ."

"I could hang out here with Pete and Sam at the studio and take an acting class or something. . . ."

"Acting class?"

"Yeah, Sam says they have some good ones and that would sort of be like going to performing arts camp, which is what I was supposed to be doing anyway?"

"Well . . . let me think about it." She then paused for a moment before saying, "Tell Pete to call me later. If it's all right with him, and if there's enough adult supervision—"

"This place is crazy with adult supervision."

"Just have him call me later."

Cooked to perfection.

That done, I checked my e-mail. There were two messages: one from Frog and one from my dad.

I opened the message from my dad first. It went like this:

Tyler,

How's La-La Land? It's hotter than blazes here. Hope Pete is taking you to some places where you might actually learn something useful. They have a great museum of science and industry. There's a car museum that is supposed to be pretty good. Whatever happened to that model-car collection you used to have? I'll bet some of those cars will be in this museum. And be sure to go to the La Brea Tar Pits. [Can you believe it? My dad just said The The Tar Tar Pits.]

I really am sorry that I couldn't have you stay with me while your mother is taking her little vacation, but I'm swamped with work and wouldn't be able to spend any quality time with you, anyway. Maybe you can come out for Labor Day.

Stay out of trouble, son.
Love,
Dad

The last thing I could tell my dad was that I'd rather be out in Hollywood with Pete right now than in New York with him, being dragged to museums and aquariums and stuff like that. Don't get me wrong, I'm not against education, but going to a museum with my dad is worse than being in school. He constantly has to be explaining what everything is, what period it's from, the social and religious atmosphere of the time, and on and on and on. He even has a way of making fun things, like sports and games, not fun. Baseball: "No, no, that's not how you do it. Here, let me show you. You see, you have to get your body in front of the ball." Or football: "How many times do I have to tell you, put your fingers on the laces. That's what they're there for." Or chess: "If you move your queen out too soon, you're going to get clobbered. I've told you that a thousand times. Come on, think, think." I'd just stare at the board. He'd then do the thing I hated most. He'd tap on my head and go, "Earth to Tyler. Earth to Tyler." I got some satisfaction knowing he had said The The Tar Tar Pits.

Then I opened Frog's e-mail. He'd done his research on Jerry Stone, and here's what he'd come up with so far:

1) Jerry Stone was Jerry Stone's real name.
2) He was born in 1958 in Indianapolis.
3) He'd lived in Chicago for five years, where he'd been a member of the Second City comedy troupe.
4) He'd been married and divorced twice. No kids.
5) He'd come out to California in the early eighties and done some commercials and small TV roles.
6) His big break was in 1986 on *Stupefried*. He played the pastry chef. The show ran for five seasons, and he'd won three Emmys for best supporting actor.
7) *Kids in the House* debuted in 1993. It became the No. 1 show in America in its second season.
8) Every film that Jerry Stone had been in had bombed.
9) Jerry was into horses. He was at the track as much as possible.
10) He'd worked as a party magician when he was first starting out in show business.
11) He'd had a hair transplant.

I thanked Frog for the info, saying I owed him big-time, gave him a quick recap of my day, and signed off. I then turned on the TV and lay back on the couch thinking about what I might say to Jerry Stone when I saw him again. I hadn't gotten further than *Mr. Stone, who's your favorite jockey?* before I fell asleep.

8

The phone conversation with my mom had been a huge success. Not only had I escaped day camp, but she'd also told Pete that she had no problem with the "rough" language I might hear in the writers' room. My mom may have been a worrier about my well-being, but she didn't feel any major threat from bad words. My dad might have had a different opinion on this, but luckily nobody was asking him. It was now okay for me to enter the writers' room from time to time.

Some people take forever to get things done. They get an idea and sit on it and maybe, sometimes, actually take action; usually not. That wasn't Sam. By the time I saw her on Thursday morning she was already gathering information on acting classes for kids. She had also made plans for getting pictures taken of me. "You can't walk in to meet a casting director without a picture and résumé," she said. "They'll laugh you out of the room."

Sam told me this as we sat in the bleachers on the soundstage watching the actors get their blocking from this week's director. Some shows had one director do most of the episodes, but *Kids in the House* was more typical, bringing in different people to direct each week. Blocking is where you move to or stand. It includes business like fumbling with the phone, or getting stuck in an air-conditioning duct, and other bits of slapstick that

Jerry Stone was brilliant at. In the late afternoon there would be a run-through, and the writers would get to see if all the stuff they had rewritten the day before was working.

The writers, meanwhile, were working on next week's script.

We weren't the only ones watching the rehearsal. There were stand-ins and extras waiting to be used and parents of some of the kid stars just waiting. Stand-in was one job that was self-descriptive. While the stars of the show studied their lines or talked to their agents or—if school was in session—did their homework, the stand-ins stood there, and the tech people figured out lighting and camera angles and stuff like that.

"Have you talked to Pete yet?" Sam asked as we stood over the craft service table, snacking.

"Not yet."

"Well, you should get on that. Like I said before, he may not jump at the idea of asking his bosses for a favor. It may take a few attempts."

Eddie McNamara was walking our way. "We should ask Eddie about acting class," Sam said. Eddie played Devin in *Kids* and was the oldest member of the Parker household. He'd been on the show since the beginning, when he was eight, and was the only kid from the original cast still on the show. I figured he had one more year before he went off to college (as Devin) and then would just come back for Thanksgiving and Christmas episodes. Who knows, he might even get a spin-off series of his own. He was incredibly popular. His face was

plastered all over the teen magazines, and he'd been fea-
tured in a number of movies over the years.

"Hey, Eddie, how's it going?" Sam cheerfully asked.

"This script blows" was Eddie's gruff response.

"This is Tyler. His uncle's one of the writers."

"Oh. Well, it still blows. Sorry, kid."

There's something weird about a seventeen-year-old
calling you kid.

Sam didn't waste any more time and got right to it:
"Who's the best acting teacher for kids?" she asked.

"I thought you hated acting."

"I do. It's for Tyler. He wants to go to a Hollywood acting class while he's out here."

"Yeah?"

"He's really funny." Sam turned to me. "Do the lobster being boiled for Eddie."

I felt funny performing for Eddie McNamara, but if I
wanted to get on the show I was going to have to get
over that kind of nervousness. So I got on the floor and
went through my routine of being reluctantly plucked
out of the lobster tank by tongs and thrown into a pot of
boiling water. Sam laughed, but Eddie just kind of
grinned and said, "Jeez, kid, don't quit your day job."
Having Eddie say that made me feel like I was two
inches tall, but Sam wasn't deterred. "So what's a good
class?" she asked.

"Thelma Bennett's. Definitely. She's tough but gets
the best out of you. I still use her for coaching."

"Thanks," we said in unison.

Eddie walked away. "What a jerk. He's like a mini

Jerry Stone. He hit on my mom at the wrap party last year. But I think he's right about Thelma Bennett. Everyone says she's the best."

"Are there any kids on the show that you like?" I asked.

"Gary's too young to be too obnoxious, but he knows he's cute so I don't give him long. Mia and Steve are pretty cool. They mostly hang out together, both on the show and off. Faith is incredibly nice, but I don't think she can handle all this fame." Faith Remo was Mexican American and played a Guatemalan fifteen-year-old. She was very pretty, and Sam said that her managers were trying to launch a career for her as a singer as well as an actress. "She never seems happy," Sam continued. "She's always crying, upset about something or other." As if on cue, Faith came running by in tears and ran out the door of the soundstage. "She what I mean?" Sam said, totally not surprised.

We found Kari talking to one of the costume ladies. "What's up with Faith?" Sam asked.

"Who knows? It doesn't take much to set her off. She's so sensitive. Poor girl," Kari said sympathetically.

"Excuse me for not feeling sorry for her," Sam said sarcastically.

"Samantha, some people have low self-esteem no matter how famous or successful they are."

"And some people have too much."

Jerry Stone was walking our way. "That girl should just go back to Guatemala," he said with irritation in his voice.

"She's from Los Angeles, Jerry," Kari corrected him.

"Yeah, whatever. These crying jags have completely gotten out of hand."

"What did you do?"

"What did *I* do? That's great, you just assume that it's my fault."

"What did you say to her?"

"She mispronounced 'foliage,' and I merely corrected her. She kept saying 'foilage'; someone had to set her straight."

"And I'm sure you did it in the kindest tone possible," Kari said. It was clear where Sam had picked up her gift for sarcasm.

"We're all supposed to be professionals here. She's getting paid as an adult. She should behave like one too." Suddenly Jerry was staring straight at me. "Well, if it isn't the kid with the cell phone."

"He has a name," Kari said. "This is Tyler. He's Pete Marcowitz's nephew."

"Who's Pete Marcowitz?"

"He's only been writing on the show for three years. He won an Emmy last year."

"Oh, *Peter* Marcowitz. Why didn't you say so?"

I was quickly getting the idea that this was a typical off-screen conversation between America's favorite on-screen couple. I caught a look from Sam that seemed to be telling me this might be a good moment to kiss up to Jerry Stone.

"Do you still do magic?" I boldly asked.

"The child has a voice," Jerry replied dryly. "Have you

been reading my unauthorized biography?" *No, I thought, but my friend Frog probably did, along with archived editions of* the National Enquirer *and* People *magazine.*

"Most of what they write about me, they make up," Jerry said casually.

"Like about having a hair transplant?" As soon as the words passed through my lips, I wanted to suck them back into my mouth and swallow them forever. The costume lady, Kari, and even Sam all had stunned expressions on their faces. Jerry Stone's own mouth tightened and then relaxed as he calmly said, "Yes, it's true. I do know a bit of magic. My specialty is making children disappear." Then he turned and walked away.

"**I** still can't believe you said that," Sam said, laughing. She had been laughing all the way from the soundstage to the production office to Pete's office, which is where we now were.

"How did I know that the one thing true about him was about his phony hair?"

"I wish I had a picture of Jerry's face when you said that. He looked like he'd swallowed a turd or something."

"Now he'll never let me be on the show," I said.

Sam's demeanor shifted from jovial to thoughtful. "Well, this isn't going to make it any easier, but we'll figure something out. We've got a long way to go before we get to Jerry giving you the okay to be in the cast."

One of the production assistants—everyone called them P.A.s—walked into the room. Her named was Bonnie. She was in her twenties and like most P.A.s worked long hours for little money just to have the opportunity to work in "the business."

"You guys want to come with me to pick up lunch?" It was ten-thirty in the morning, but to make sure the writers had their lunches by twelve-thirty or one, Bonnie had to take their orders now. This was Bonnie's second season as a P.A. on *Kids*, and by now she knew what every writer ordered from every restaurant in the area.

Still, every day the writers would go through the same ritual: Someone would pick a restaurant (they usually rotated), then Bonnie would give everyone photocopied menus from the selected eatery, followed by the writers looking over the menus for a few minutes and then ordering whatever it was they ordered every time that particular restaurant was chosen. On the drive over to that day's selection, the Out Take Café, we quizzed Bonnie on each writer's food preferences.

"All right, let's see . . . Pete from the Daily Grill?" Sam asked.

Without hesitation Bonnie launched into it: "Turkey meat loaf with green beans, and a salad with ranch dressing on the side."

"Baxter, from Chin Chin."

"Chinese chicken salad and Szechuan dumplings."

"Sherry, from California Pizza Kitchen."

"Chicken Caesar salad. Dressing on the side. No croutons. She has a problem with gluten."

"What's gluten?" I asked.

"I'm not exactly sure but she can't eat bread. Some sort of digestive problem."

While we were waiting for the food at the Out Take Café, my cell phone went off. It took me a moment to figure out it was mine because it seemed like they were going off all over the place the whole time we were there. It was my mom, of course. She was having second thoughts about me not being in day camp and was probably afraid I'd fallen into a pit of mischief.

"Tyler, did you tell your father what you were doing?"

"I thought if it was okay with you then it would be—"

"How many times have we talked about not playing one of us against the other?"

"But—"

"Your father and I may disagree on a lot of things, but we're of one mind on this. Now, you call him tonight and make sure he approves."

"Okay."

"Good. Are you having fun?"

"Yeah, Mom."

"Raphael says you should have Pete take you to Magic Mountain."

Our massive food order was being placed on the counter.

"I gotta go, Mom."

"I love you, honey."

"Bye."

I hated my mom's second thoughts. All the work and careful timing to get her to the correct first thought, and then she has to go and have a second thought. Don't get me wrong. I know as a parent you have to be thinking all the time, and her point about me not wanting to tell my dad about skipping day camp was exactly right, but there would be no way my dad would have said yes, so I figured it was better to move forward and tell him later, and that way he'd see there was no harm done. Right? If I could just put off telling him for a day or two, he might get mad, really mad, but I'd be on my way to getting on the show.

Everyone seemed to have an idea about what I should be doing, even stupid old Raphael. My dad thought I should be at camp and going to car museums. My mom just wanted to be sure that I wasn't having an asthma attack somewhere on the back lot of Universal Studios or getting my feelings crushed because of unrealistic expectations.

We got back to the *Kids* production offices and hauled the food up to the writers' room.

Sam went off to use the phone while Bonnie and I distributed the food. She rejoined me just as I was about to walk into Pete's office to give him his lunch.

"Okay, here's the deal," Sam said. "Thelma Bennett will let you take her class this Saturday, but she wants Pete to come in and talk to her *actors*." Sam said the word "actors" as if she were some grand dame of the American theater. "She also wanted my mom to come to the class. I told her that I was sure she'd love to—someday."

We entered Pete's office, and I gave him his Cobb salad and root beer. I was beginning to get really good at picking up on Sam's looks. This time her eyes said, *Talk to him about getting you an audition,* while her mouth said, "I'm gonna see what my mom's doing."

"I didn't realize I was starving," Pete said. He put a forkful of Cobb salad into his mouth while I chomped down on my cheeseburger. "Hey, listen," he said, "you have to call your dad and make sure he's okay with you spending all your time here at the studio."

"Yeah, I know. Mom called while we were getting the food."

I should tell you something about my dad and Pete: They don't like each other very much. Even when we were all a family, they never seemed to have anything to say to each other. When Pete was working at the video store and doing stand-up, my dad thought he was a total loser. He'd say to my mom, "The guy should be doing something useful with his life. He's going to end up alone and broke. Do you want me to talk to him?" This would make my mom incredibly mad, and she'd launch into one of her "You think you know what's best for everyone" speeches, which would be followed by a "You're totally overreacting, as usual" from my dad. From there, my mom would then compare my dad to a brick wall, or a slab of cement, or some other impenetrable surface. Now that Pete was a successful TV writer, my dad still couldn't say that he might have been wrong about Pete. In fact, I can't remember my dad ever saying he was wrong or even sorry about something he did or said. His most common method of apology was taking us out for hot fudge sundaes. At best he'd say that Pete was working in the lowest form of entertainment, television, and that TV only promoted laziness and stupidity. At worst he'd say it wouldn't be long before Pete was back in the video store, Emmy or no Emmy. And I guess that was Pete's fear, as well, and why he kept his crummy old car and apartment.

"Do you think I might be able to audition for the show?" I bluntly asked.

Pete continued chewing and after a moment said, "Well, I don't know; it's not that simple."

"How come?"

"Well, first of all, the kids you see out there all have agents, and this is for a big part, so we're really looking for kids with some experience. . . ."

"I'm going to take a class with Teresa Barrett."

"Do you mean Thelma Bennett?"

"Yeah, her."

"I hear her classes are really hard to get into. Not to mention expensive."

"But she said if you came and talked to the class, she'd let me in this Saturday for free. Sam set it up."

"Sam?"

"Yeah."

"I don't know, Tyler, I usually don't like to . . ."

I quickly worked my face into a puppy dog expression that had often worked for me in the past when dealing with adults. Who says I can't act?

"All right," Pete said. "We'll go to the class on Saturday, but as far as an audition goes, I don't want you to get your hopes up. I'll see what I can do."

My hopes were up. Way up. I decided not to let them come crashing to the ground by doing anything dangerous like telling my dad I wasn't at the Y.

Sometimes the truth can ruin everything.

10

The next day was Friday, and late in the afternoon there would be a network run-through, at which time everyone from the network or studio could give Baxter Rhodes their two cents. After that, the writers would go back and do another rewrite, this time with the aid of Neal Peachy, who came in to help punch up the script.

Sam had her tennis lesson on Friday mornings, so I asked Pete if I could hang out in the writers' room and he said it would be okay.

The writers had split in half. One group was working on next week's script, and the other had gone off to another room to break an upcoming story. That was the group Pete was in. Most of the time I sat there, I felt like I was in another country. What I mean is, the writers used terms and had a way of talking that only *they* seemed to understand. I asked Pete about it, and he said to write down anything I didn't know and he'd tell me what it meant if I hadn't figured it out on my own.

Here's the list I assembled and the definitions Pete gave me:

1) Laying the Pipe—The pipe gets you to the heart of the story. Say, in the story about Grace's birth mother showing up, a bit of pipe might be Grace

getting on the Internet and finding a service that trails adoptions.

2) Tracking—The writers want to make sure that every story follows a logical progression. If it isn't, they might say "the camping story isn't tracking."

3) House Number—Sometimes a writer will have an idea for a joke but hasn't quite figured it out how to make it funny. Before he makes his pitch, he might say "house number." It's warning the other writers that he's going to fill in something, probably lame, until the real joke comes along.

4) Hang a Lantern on It—If a plot point or a joke is really obvious, you hang a lantern on it, meaning by overemphasizing it, you let the audience know that you (the writers) know it's a lame joke or a big coincidence or whatever.

5) Burying the Pipe—Making it so the audience doesn't see how you're stringing together the bits of information that are leading to a main story point.

6) Plot-o-gram—When a writer suggests a big piece of plot that seems to come out of nowhere, one of the other writers in the room might knock on the table (or go "ding-dong") and say "plot-o-gram."

7) House of Buys—Similar to plot-o-gram, only someone goes "ring-ring," mimes picking up the phone, and says "house of buys."

8) Bumping—If someone in the room is having trouble with the logic of the story, they might say "I'm bumping on that."
9) The Blow—The last line or action of a scene or an act. In sitcoms you almost always want the blow to be a big laugh line.
10) Runner—A joke that gets repeated and built on throughout the episode.
11) Clam (or Clammy)—A really bad joke. Makes you feel like you just ate some bad clams.
12) Nakamura—The legend of this term goes like this: Once, during a taping of *The Bob Newhart Show*, there was a runner that had to do with a Mr. Nakamura. Well, according to the story, the first time they used the joke, not one person in the audience laughed—which meant that the rest of the Mr. Nakamura jokes were *all* going to bomb. So if on a tape night the first running joke chokes, you know you're in trouble.

Even though I couldn't follow a lot of what was going on in the room, it was fun just to be there.

The network run-through went pretty well. At these run-throughs, as with the taping, the writers, director, and network and studio people would move in a pack and stand behind the cameras at whatever part of the set was being used. There were a lot more laughs at the run-through than at the table-read. Pete and the other writers would make little check marks in their scripts for material that worked and *X*s for stuff that didn't. I managed to stay out of Jerry Stone's way the whole time. After the run-through, Baxter Rhodes and the other high-end writers got notes from the network and studio execs, and Jerry Stone.

I had just walked out of the soundstage to go back to the production bungalow when someone yelled, "Hey, kid, catch." I looked up just in time to see a football spiraling down toward my head. I made the catch. Eddie McNamara said, "Good one, kid," and I tossed the ball back to him. Two of the P.A.s, Greg and Pat, were also playing catch, and for the next twenty minutes or so we heaved the ball back and forth, careful not to hit any of the cars that were parked in the area. Pete and Ellen, another one of the writers, came out after a while and joined in. It was great. For me, tossing a football around was one of those activities that seemed to make you feel like you belonged. What I mean is, here were the writers of the show, one of the biggest teen stars in the country, a couple of production assistants, and me all having a great old time without a worry in the world.

The writers got off early that night. Pete said that once they got further into the season, it would become rarer and rarer to get off at six P.M., which was what time it was when we left the studio. He asked me if I'd like to have enchiladas for dinner. This was Pete's specialty. Actually, it was about the only thing I'd ever seen him cook. We were in the Hughes Market on Ventura Boulevard throwing enchilada makings into the cart when my cell phone went off. I was expecting my mom on the other end, but it was Sam. I'd forgotten that I'd given her the number.

"What are you doing tonight?" she asked.

"Pete's making enchiladas." I then had a thought. "Hold on a sec."

"Can I invite Sam to dinner?" I called out to Pete, who was selecting green peppers.

"Sure," he said.

"You wanna come over?" I asked Sam.

"Yeah, but how am I gonna get there?"

"We'll come and get you." And then to Pete, "Can we pick Sam up?"

Pete was saying "sure," and at the same time Sam was saying, "Wait, I've got a better idea. Hang on." Sam then screamed to her mom, asking if she wanted to have dinner with us. A moment later she came back on the line. "Ask Pete if my mom can come too."

"Okay," I said. Pete had moved on to the red peppers. "Can her mom come too?"

From the look on Pete's face, you'd think I'd asked him to jump out of an airplane.

"Kari wants to come too?"

"Yeah."

"Okay," he said calmly, entirely missing the cart he had intended to drop the peppers into.

"Fine with him," I told Sam.

"Cool. What time should we come over and how do we get there?"

.   .   .

Pete had made his enchiladas maybe, I don't know, a million times but was preparing everything like he'd never done it before. He was also doing stuff I'd never seen him do, like vacuum and put the toilet seat in its down position. He took his Emmy out of the refrigerator and spent about ten minutes trying to find the right place for it. He finally settled for a spot in one of the bookcases.

"You're nervous because of Kari, huh?" I said to Pete as he carefully filled a tortilla with simmering sauce and grated cheese.

"No, of course not."

"Sam thinks you have a crush on her mom."

"Well, not exactly a crush. I mean, a crush sounds like I'm in high school or something."

"So you're in love with her?"

"No, no, no. I'll go with crush. Strange word, huh? Crush? It implies destruction and devastation. It could also be some sort of secret organization. Like ..." (in a Russian accent) "I am from C.R.U.S.H., here to make mincemeat of all your romantic aspirations."

"And C.R.U.S.H. could stand for Committee to Ruin ..."

"Unwarranted Sophomoric Hopes."

"What's sophomoric?"

"It's when you're an adult and you act like you're in high school."

The enchiladas were a big hit with everyone, though Sam only ate the cheese variety because she didn't eat meat. "If you knew the conditions they breed these animals in, you'd stop eating it too," she said with disgust.

"At least a fish gets to enjoy a life in an ocean or river before becoming someone's dinner. For a cow it's like living in a penitentiary from birth to death." I pictured a cow sitting in Joliet Prison, a guard slipping him a plate of grass under the door. "We're from Chicago," Pete said. "When we say we're breast-fed, we're talking brisket." That one went over Sam's head—I guess she didn't know her cuts of beef—but Kari laughed.

"Who wants a tarot reading?" Kari asked after we'd maxed out on enchiladas.

"Mom, what are you doing?" Sam asked in disbelief.

"I just thought Pete and Tyler might want to see what's in their future."

"But you never get anything right," Sam said.

"Excuse me, didn't the cards tell you that you'd unexpectedly lose something of value, and the next week you lost your appendix?"

"That is such a stretch," Sam groaned. "Anyway, who values their appendix?"

"Well, it sure cost enough to have it removed. Besides, it's just for fun. Who wants to go first?"

I definitely wanted to know what my future was and quickly volunteered. Kari asked me to think of a question while I shuffled the deck of tarot cards she had pulled from her purse. She said I didn't have to say it out loud if I didn't want to. I didn't want to. My question was: Will I get a part on *Kids in the House*?

"Oh my, these are very interesting," Kari said after laying ten cards on the table.

"What do they say?" I anxiously asked.

"Well, this card here ..." Kari was pointing to a card that showed a man carrying a bunch of sticks. He seemed to be having a tough time. "This means that there's something you're struggling with."

"Duh," said Sam.

"I foresee back trouble in your future, Tyler. Remember to always lift with your legs," Pete joked.

"It could mean you're feeling the weight of the world or some sort of burden—"

"Or that you're going camping soon," Sam interrupted.

"That's enough from you two. Now, this card represents your past." Kari tapped on a card showing a burning tower with people jumping out of it. "This is a major card and usually indicates some huge upheaval in a person's life. In this case it might be your parents' divorce."

"Nice guess, Mom, but they got divorced a million years ago," Sam said.

"Is this reading for you, young lady? When you've been in therapy as long as I have, you learn that there are some things you never get over. Isn't that right, Pete?"

"It's true. I'm still reeling from coming in last in the Pinewood Derby in Cub Scouts."

"What's a Pinewood Derby?" asked Sam.

"It's a competition in the Cub Scouts where the fathers and sons are supposed to build a race car together out of, well, pinewood. I come from a long line of mechanically challenged males, and our car was so slow it didn't even make it to the finish line. It would have moved faster if we'd just thrown the block of wood onto the track."

Sam and Kari were laughing at Pete's story when my eyes fixed on a tarot card that looked like the world, surrounded by all sorts of stuff. "What's this card?" I asked. The others stopped talking, and Kari looked at the card I was pointing at. "That's the Wheel of Fortune," she began. "And it's in your future. It's what we call the outcome. There could be a tremendous opportunity coming up for you." I knew she had to be talking about a part on the show. "But," she continued, "you have to be very observant, because sometimes the opportunity may not be the one we're hoping for or expecting." I wasn't sure what she meant by this but I didn't ask. To me it was obvious. I was going to be the next cast member of *Kids in the House*. The only other thing that stuck out for me was a card that had a man on a throne with a sword in his hand. He looked really mean.

"Hey, it's Jerry Stone," Sam said.

Kari ignored her daughter. "That is the King of Swords; he could be a real obstacle for you or he could be an ally."

"I guess you covered all your bases there," Sam wisecracked.

"The King of Swords is usually bright and can be very domineering," Kari continued. "Not so much in a physical way, but someone who always thinks they're right and knows what's best for everyone else."

"Sounds like your dad," Pete said. "Doesn't it, Tyler?"

I nodded. "That's him, all right," I said.

Maybe it was the enchiladas, but I suddenly got a sick feeling in the pit of my stomach.

11

Thelma Bennett's acting class was on Saturday morning. We pulled into a huge apartment complex off Barham Boulevard—Pete, Sam, and me. It was called the Oakwood Apartments and was sort of a center for aspiring kid actors. Parents would bring their children from all over the country so that the kids could take classes with people like Thelma Bennett, have meetings with agents or managers, go to cattle-call auditions, and stay for anywhere from a week to "as long as it takes for my kid to get a break."

Thelma Bennett's class was held in one of the rec rooms. Thelma herself was in her sixties. She had platinum blond hair, a tight crinkly face with intense brown eyes, and an air about her that made you think you'd just met someone of royal persuasion. To make the effect even stronger, she sat in a great high-backed leather chair that looked like a throne, while everyone else sat in folding chairs. A girl of about sixteen was standing in front of her with an anguished look on her face when we walked in. As we approached, we caught the end of their conversation.

"The woman I talked to just said that he wasn't taking on any new clients right now," the girl was saying.

"And you told them I'd referred you?" Thelma said, intensely focused on the girl.

"Yes. Several times."

"Unbelievable!" Thelma said with theatrical exasperation. She then pulled a cell phone out of her chair/throne and hit what I guessed was a speed-dial button. "Jeff, Thelma Bennett here." There was a brief pause and then Thelma continued: "I don't care if it's goddamn Christmas. When I send a student to you, I don't expect them to be brushed aside like some lint off your Armani suit." There was another brief pause and then: "I don't care how many of *her type* you think you have, this girl is going to make some agent a lot of money, and I thought I'd give you the opportunity to be the one building an extension onto his house and not someone else." Another pause and then: "All right, I'll tell her. Thank you, dear. Love to Karen. Bye bye." Thelma looked up at the girl. "Call on Monday. He'll see you next week."

The girl threw her arms around Thelma. "Oh, thank you, Thelma. You're the best." Thelma peeled the girl off. "Now don't go in there and forget everything I've taught you. Enough. Go. Sit." The girl made her way to the other students, who numbered about fifteen and were now taking their seats. Thelma stood for the first time. "You must be Peter Marcowitz," she said, holding out her arm to Pete, who looked like he wasn't sure whether he should shake her hand or kiss her ring. Thelma solved his dilemma by grabbing Pete's hand and shaking it.

"Just Pete is fine. Nice to meet you," he said. "This is Tyler and Samantha."

"I'm just watching," said Sam.

"Samantha Franklin, yes, you're the one who called me about this young man taking the class," Thelma said, gesturing toward me. "Did you ask your mother if she'd like to come by and speak to my students sometime?"

"Not yet, but I'm sure she'd love to when she has a little more time." For someone who didn't want to act, Sam was pretty good.

"Wonderful!" Thelma exclaimed. She then turned to Pete. "What have you prepared for us today, Peter?"

"Just Pete is fine. I thought I'd just talk a little about how we put the show together each week, and about the process that goes on between the writers and actors."

"Perfect." She turned back to Sam and me. "Why don't you two have a seat while Peter talks to the class."

"Nobody really calls me—" but Thelma had already pivoted toward her students. Sam and I took seats as Thelma introduced him: "Peter Marcowitz, supervising producer from *Kids in the House*." Everyone clapped as Thelma sat back on her throne. She then gave a final decree to her subjects: "Now, this *not* an audition! When we do our scene work today, I want you to approach it exactly the same as if nobody from TV's most popular show were in the room."

"Yeah, right," Sam whispered to me sarcastically.

"Hey, everybody," Pete said. "I've got a joke for you." Pete launched into one of the thousand or so jokes he knew. It was a talking dog joke. He had a lot of those. I'm sure he picked it because it was clean and it had to do with show business: "This guy walks into a talent

61

agent's office with his dog, and the agent asks what he can do for him. The guy says his dog can talk, and the agent says, 'Sure, sure, all right, let's see what he can do,' so the guy turns to his dog, points to the ceiling and says, 'What's that?' and the dog barks, 'Rrroof.' The agent doesn't look impressed, so the guy takes the dog's paw and rubs it against his own chin and says, 'How does that feel?' The dog barks, 'Rrrough.' The agent says, 'Come on, buddy. I haven't got all day.' The guy says, 'You're gonna love this next one,' and he asks the dog, 'Who's the greatest ballplayer that ever lived?' The dog barks, 'Rrruth.' The guy looks at the agent, who says, 'Sorry, buddy, your dog stinks.' So the guy and dog walk out of the office. They get on an elevator and the dog goes, 'Maybe I should have said Ken Griffey, Jr.' "
Everyone laughed.

Pete spent the next ten minutes telling everyone about how the writers put the show together each week and how they developed the characters. He then opened the floor to questions. You could tell that Thelma had these kids well trained in what was appropriate or inappropriate to ask her guest speakers.

"Mr. Marcowitz, what do you and the other producers of *Kids in the House* like to see when someone comes in for an audition?" a girl of about fifteen asked.

"Well, on the one hand we're looking for someone who fits the part the way we've written it. Someone who can find all the laughs and hit those lines. But we also look for people who can bring their own uniqueness into the role. That's especially true with the ongoing characters, because that way the character truly becomes a collaboration between actor and writer."

"What have I been telling you?" Thelma broke in. "*You* are your most valuable asset. *You* are what no other actor has. Never leave *you* in the waiting room or *you* will be unemployed."

The next question came from another girl of about thirteen. "What's the worst thing someone can do in an audition?"

Pete thought about that one for a second and then said, "Cry."

Again Thelma burst in: "You see? Old Thelma hasn't been teaching the future young stars of America for the last thirty-five years for just her health. Tears from an actor, unless called for in the script, will only bring you one thing in this town. And what is it?"

"Unemployment," the class said in unison.

"Precisely!"

There were a few more rounds of questions and applause for Pete, and then Thelma had us do a physical and vocal warm-up, followed by some improvisations. For these, she'd select two or three students, set up a situation—like a boy and a girl on their first date—and then say, "Action." The actors would then totally make up the scene.

The improvisation I did was with another boy, Todd, who was about sixteen or seventeen. Thelma told us that we were brothers whose mom was in the hospital. She told me that I was in the hospital waiting room. She then whispered something to Todd, who nodded, and then got ready to enter. Thelma said, "Action!" Todd started to walk slowly toward me. He looked serious. It was obvious that he was going to tell me that our mom had died, and then I'd have to improvise how a kid would act upon hearing that news. I figured that if I cried—called for in the scene, like Thelma had said—everyone would be impressed. I remembered something Sam had said earlier that day: "If you have to cry, think of something really sad from your own life. If that doesn't work, pull a hair out of your nose."

As Todd was saying, "I've got something I need to tell you," I searched my memory for something sad: my dog, Quaker, dying? I didn't feel a thing. Losing the Little League championship game the year before? Nope, nothing. I went for one that my real mom and her therapist thought I should have cried buckets over: her and my dad's divorce. Sorry, eyes still dry.

"It's about Mom . . . ," Todd said. I turned my back to the audience, quickly finding a nose hair with my thumb and forefinger, and yanked as hard as I could. I then turned back to Todd. "She had a baby girl," he said. Tears were streaming down my face. I was in pain. I was speechless. I was bleeding. I heard a few giggles, though my eyes were too filled with tears to know where they were coming from. Todd kept right on going: "What's the matter? Aren't you happy? What's wrong with your nose?" By now I could hear snippets of laughter throughout the room. All I could think to say was "I think I'm having a brain hemorrhage." The entire room burst into laughter.

"Cut!" Thelma mercifully said. "I think we can all thank young Mr. Stewart not only for pointing out the pitfalls of self-mutilation on stage, but for an invaluable lesson: Never get so lost in acting that you forget to *react* to what's *really* going on."

Sam was still laughing as we lapped up our triple scoop cones at the 31 Flavors in Toluca Lake. "That was the funniest thing I've ever seen," she snorted.

"You were the one who told me to pull a nose hair out."

"Yeah, I said *a* nose hair, not an entire forest of them, plus some skin."

Besides the nose-hair improvisation, I had been asked to read a scene from *To Kill a Mockingbird*. Perhaps you've seen it or even read the book. I was hoping to get to do a funny scene, but I guess Thelma figured I'd gotten enough laughs already. This was a scene where Jem (that's me) shows Scout all the things that Boo Radley has been leaving him in the knothole of the old tree in front of their house. There's some marbles and a broken pocket watch, a spelling medal, and two dolls (that look just like Jem and Scout) carved out of soap. As we read the scene, I did my best to follow Thelma's advice of listening and reacting.

I must have done something in that scene that convinced Pete that I had some acting ability, because he said, "I'll see if I can get you in for an audition next week." I was about to bust out of my skin, but then he added, "You're going to have to clear it first with your mom and dad." I took a deep breath, or at least tried to. Air was coming in at about 80 percent. I gave myself a blast from my inhaler. "You okay, pal?" Pete asked.

"I'm fine," I said, nodding and giving myself another blast.

12

We dropped Sam off at her house and headed home on the 101 Freeway. I didn't know what to do. I figured my mom would have no problem with me auditioning for *Kids*, but my dad was another story. He had seen too many *E! True Hollywood Story* shows on child actors and was sure that a trip to stardom also meant a trip to drug rehab, or jail, or years on Dr. Von Headshrinker's couch. Probably all of the above. My plan had been to tell him *after* I'd gotten the part, but Pete was making that hard. If I told my mom, she'd feel obligated to tell my dad, and that would be the end of Tyler Stewart's television career. She'd taken my side against my dad before, but I was pretty sure she wouldn't fight him on this.

I could plead my case to Pete, asking him to do the tried-and-true adult delaying tactic: wait and see. *Can't we wait to see if I get the part, and if I do, then tell them?* No, it would never work. Pete may have been fun and all that, but he would never keep my mom out of the loop on something like this.

I thought of something that my dad always said about taking a case to court: "If you present your case in the correct manner, you have a better chance of getting the results you want; to do that, you've got to know who's sitting in the jury box."

Here's how I got my dad to say it was okay for me to

audition for *Kids:* I turned it into a lesson. I called him as soon as we got home. He was happy to hear from me.

"Has Pete taken you over to the Museum of Science and Industry?" he asked.

"Not yet."

"How about the La Brea Tar Pits?"

I was tempted to tell him about The The Tar Tar Pits, but I knew it wasn't the right time. "No, not yet," I said. "I wanted to see if it's okay if I audition for a part on *Kids in the House.*"

"Definitely out of the question."

"That's what I thought," I calmly replied. "I just thought I'd check. There's no way that they're going to give me a part anyway. There's kids with agents and managers, and they stay at the Oakwood Apartments and take acting classes and all they do is audition, but I figured since I was here it might be a good thing to get out of my system."

Getting things out of your system is a very adult thing to do. How many times have you been in the next room and overheard your parents talking about you, saying stuff like: *Don't worry about it. It's just a phase. Let him get it out of his system.* There was a bit of a pause, and then my dad said, "That's a very mature way to look at this. If it's all right with your mother, then it's all right with me. Call me after your audition and we'll discuss this." *We'll discuss what you've learned* is what he meant.

Having my dad on board made getting my mom's

approval a cinch. She was more concerned about my expectations being too high than about the evils of Hollywood. "There are so many things beyond your control. Just go in there and do your best. It's an honor just to audition," she said, obviously confusing the old Oscar line ("It's an honor just to be nominated!") with my chance to read for the producers of *Kids*. "Oh, honey, Raphael wants to say something to you."

Great! Now I had to get advice from Raphael.

I should tell you a little something about Raphael. He's a model that my mom met when the advertising agency she works for hired him to do some print ads for Neiman Marcus. "He's a real Italian," my mom said to me while getting ready for her first date with him. "He's only been in our wonderful country a few months but has made a great many friends." *Terrific, I thought, you just met the guy and you're quoting him, bad English and all.* Raphael was good-looking, I'll give him that. He was younger than my mom by about ten years and her first real boyfriend since the divorce. I'd seen enough made-for-TV movies to know that he was a transitional boyfriend and it would never last. Still, he bugged me. He was too friendly, too eager to show my mom how much he liked me. Whatever. I just didn't need his advice on anything, and now his Italian accent was on the other end of the phone saying: "Tyler, how ya doin', my man?"

"Great, Raphael."

"Good, good. Listen, I want to tell you something for

your audition. You remember this and you got no problems. They will love you."

"What is it?"

"Give them your teeth."

"What?"

"Don't forget to smile. You smile, they know you're not afraid."

They'll know I'm not afraid? I felt like I was getting advice from someone in a Mafia movie.

"Okay, I'll smile."

"Attaboy—here's your mom."

My mom came back on: "Now, call me as soon as it's over. I want to hear everything. Oh, and have your inhaler nearby; you know how you get when you're nervous."

"I'll be fine, Mom. I'll call you after the audition."

"Good luck, honey. I love you."

In the background Raphael shouted, "And don't forget your teeth."

That evening Pete and I ate pizza and watched a couple of old movie comedies, *Ghostbusters* and *Wayne's World*. Pete told me a bit more about the part I'd be auditioning for: a kid who had gone from home to home because he was always causing trouble, mostly by stealing stuff and then lying about it or by trying to always act like a big shot around other kids.

Pete told me not to get my hopes up too high. They'd be looking at a lot of kids who had a lot more experience and training than I had. Kids who had agents and managers and pictures and résumés. It was almost the same speech I had given my dad.

There wasn't much I could do about getting an agent over the weekend, but I wouldn't be walking into my audition without a picture and résumé. Sam would help me see to that.

13

The next morning Pete dropped me off at Sam's before heading out to the golf course to get in a round with some of his old stand-up buddies.

Sam had transformed the den of her house into what looked like a photographer's studio. There were light fixtures and screens set up and several expensive-looking cameras sitting on stools. I guess when your mom earns a ton of money from being America's favorite mom, you have hobbies at twelve that look like some people's careers at forty. I should have known, though, that it was more than a hobby for Sam. For Sam it was all part of a plan. As I was learning, she always had a plan. "Eventually I'm going to get into directing, make my own movies," Sam said. I was sitting on one of the stools, and Sam was snapping off photos. "All you have to do to be a good director is not be afraid of telling people what to do." As if to prove her point, she then said, "Turn toward me. Okay, now give me a confident look." I sort of half-smiled, squinting my eyes.

"You look like an elf on cold medication. No, I mean an 'I just got a part on a TV show and I am so-o-o cool' look." I imagined myself walking into school and everyone looking at me in admiration. "That's it," Sam said, and the camera went *click*.

"Of course, you also have to know what you're

72

doing," Sam continued. "That's why I'm learning photography. It's good for my composition skills."

"You mean like writing stuff for school?"

"Photographic composition. What's in a picture; how you frame it. If you're going to make movies, you have to think in pictures."

"Hey, maybe someday I'll be in one of your movies."

"Yeah, I might let you audition."

This made me laugh, and as I did, Sam snapped off another picture.

For the next twenty minutes Sam took pictures. I even went into another room and changed shirts a couple of times for different looks.

Not only did Sam have a ton of photographic equipment, she had a darkroom where she knew how to develop the pictures she took. She developed proof sheets first. A proof sheet has tiny versions of all your photos. You look at them through a loupe, which is that thing a jeweler puts up to his eye to determine if the diamond ring you need to pawn is worth a million bucks or is a fake. I learned that in a movie.

Sam and I went into the kitchen and began looking over the proof sheets, picking out our favorites. Kari came in and joined us at the table where the proof sheets were spread out. She carefully looked at the photos. "This is good," she said. "Oh, and I like this one. It really shows off that wonderful smile of yours." She set down the loupe for a moment and looked at Sam. "So talented, so talented. And beautiful—"

"Mom," Sam interrupted.

"Though I really think you should let your hair grow out," she said, stroking Sam's hair.

"I like it this way," Sam said. For several moments Kari continued to look at her daughter, whose attention was back on one of the proof sheets. She then returned the loupe to her eye and leaned over one of the sheets. Suddenly she said, "There. There's your best shot." Sam and I checked out the photo she was pointing at. "It shows off that great smile, and there's a little twinkle in your eye. That's the one."

Sam agreed that Kari's selection was probably the best. She then developed it into an eight-by-ten photo. I now had a "head shot."

That done, we went to the computer in Sam's room and started working on my résumé.

"The key to putting together a good résumé is making everything you've ever done look better than it really was," Sam explained. "You can use this same principle when you write your autobiography."

First, we made a stop at tylertown.com. Sam thought we might find something useful there. She was immediately impressed with my Web site. Bob, the guy my dad had gotten to create the site, had it set up like a village. The first thing you saw when you came onto the site was a big sign that said:

Welcome to Tylertown
Population: 1

There was an arcade where you could play computer games. We avoided the temptation to go in there and instead went into the art gallery. Here you could look at photographs of my family and me, as well as some of my friends.

"Your parents are good-looking, especially your dad," Sam said.

"Yeah, I guess."

"What happened to you?"

"Ha ha!"

"Who's this?"

We were looking at a photo of a plump kid with black glasses who was wearing a *South Park* T-shirt.

"That's my best friend, Frog."

"He's the one who knows so much about movies and TV, right?"

"Um-hm."

"How come you call him Frog?"

"His family has a swimming pool, and when he was really little he'd just sit there on one of the steps, half in the water, half out, so his sister called him Frog. Now that's what everyone calls him, even though his real name is Harold."

We then entered the village's movie theater, from which you could download videos of me doing some of my routines. Not only did you get me doing my crazy legs and boiled lobster bits, but you could also see me as surfer dude, amnesia man, and Sam's favorite, duck out of water.

"This is all stuff we can call film work," Sam said

after watching me for the third time get out of Frog's pool and waddle around quacking.

"Let's do your résumé," Sam said.

We left Tylertown and went into the word processor. In large bold letters at the top of the page she wrote TYLER STEWART.

"Okay, let's start with your vital statistics."

She typed in my height, weight, and color of my hair and eyes.

"Have you ever been in any plays?"

"No. Well, one time our fourth-grade class read 'Rumpelstiltskin' and I got to be Rumpelstiltskin."

"Great." Under the headings *Play* and *Role*, Sam typed in "Rumpelstiltskin." "What was the name of your school?"

"Adlai Stevenson Elementary School."

"We'll call it the Stevenson Center for the Arts." She typed it in under *Theater*. "What else?"

I just shrugged.

"We'll come back to this. Let's move on."

The videos we had watched of me on my Web site went onto the résumé as *Short Films*.

"What else?"

"That's it, unless you count the newspaper ad I did when I was really little."

"You were in a print ad?"

"Yeah, but I don't remember it. I was only two."

"What was it for?"

"A clothing ad for OshKosh B'Gosh. But I was just a baby. Does that count?"

"Of course it counts. Everything counts, and especially you having done professional print work. Nobody has to know you had diapers on underneath."

"But what if someone asks about it?"

"Nobody will, but if they do just say you did it a few years ago."

Under *Training* Sam wrote in Thelma Bennett's name.

"Do you have any special skills?"

"Special skills?"

"Yeah, do you speak German or French or are you great on skis or skateboards...?"

"I'm pretty good at chess. My dad taught me."

"I don't think chess counts as a special skill."

There was a tap on the door and Kari popped her head in.

"Mom, why do you even bother to knock when you never wait for an answer?"

"Was I interrupting something?"

"No, but you might wait for me to say okay."

"Well, I wasn't knocking; I was tapping. If I were knocking, I'd be saying 'I have no idea what you're doing in there; is it all right to come in?' Whereas with a tap I'm saying 'I know what you're doing and I'm coming in, but I'll first give you this little warning as a courtesy.'"

"Unbelievable!" Sam said to no one in particular. "When's dinner?"

"In about half an hour." Kari left the room, closing the door behind her.

"Did I mention my mother's insane? What else have you done?"

"I took piano lessons for two years."

"Great." Under *Special Skills* Sam typed in "Musical: piano and singing."

Sam thought maybe Frog might remember some stuff I had done that could go on the résumé, so we called him up. Frog's voice came out of the speaker-phone: "Hello."

"Hey, man, it's Tyler. What's up?"

"Tyler, are you a star yet?"

"Not quite. That's why we need your help."

"We?"

"Yeah, Sam's here. I told you about her. Kari Franklin's daughter."

"Hey, Frog," Sam said.

After a slight pause Frog nervously said "Hello."

"What are you doing?" Sam asked.

There was a long pause. I should mention that Frog is not exactly the most social kid you're going to meet and totally uncomfortable around girls, let alone a girl who's the daughter of a TV star.

"Sam's not really a *girl* girl—" I said.

"Thanks a lot," Sam jumped in, shooting me a look.

"No, I mean, you can talk to her like . . . I'm talking to you. She's really cool."

That seemed to satisfy Sam, who then said, "Hey, Frog, we're writing a résumé for Tyler. Can you think of any funny stuff he's done that we might be able to use?"

Frog was happy to have something to focus on other than himself. He quickly set his computer-like brain into search mode. He named several of my previously mentioned routines before moving on to something I had omitted telling Sam: "You were really funny as Cinderella."

"Don't you mean *in Cinderella?*" Sam asked.

"No. Tyler *was* Cinderella."

The summer before, Frog and I were in day camp at the YMCA, and they were going to do *Cinderella*. I auditioned for the title role, just for a laugh, but everyone laughed so much that they decided I should do the part. I ad-libbed half of my dialogue and towered over Prince Charming when we danced at the ball. It was the most laughs I'd ever gotten in one place. However, after the show I was called all sorts of names by Marc Wilkey and his (in the words of Frog) "dumb as a post" gang. You know the sort of names.

Frog came to my defense: "All the great comedians have worn dresses: Milton Berle, Jim Carrey..." Then they were calling Frog names too and saying all sorts of disgusting things about the two of us that I won't repeat here. I never get into fights, but before I knew what I was doing, I had shoved Marc Wilkey onto the ground and we were swinging wildly at each other. It didn't last long, because one of the Y counselors separated us. When I got home, my mom took one look at my swollen lip and started to freak out. She was ready to call Marc Wilkey's mother, or the YMCA, or my dad and tell him to call Marc Wilkey's father, but I begged her not to. When she finally saw that I wasn't really hurt, she calmed down. After I'd told her what happened, she said, "You stood up for yourself and I'm proud of you. But next time do it without the fistfight. Those boys were just jealous because of all the attention you were getting, especially from the girls." When I talked to my dad later that night, he tried to act all responsible, saying, "Physical violence should be a person's last resource, son," but he also couldn't help asking, "So, did you win?"

"Win what?"

"The fight."

"I don't know. It all happened so fast."

"Did you remember what I taught you about fighting? Did you keep your hands up and lead with your left?" For the next five minutes I got an over-the-phone boxing lesson, capped with another "Violence is wrong and should only be used as a last resort."

I'd felt pretty good about standing up for myself but now I felt like I had somehow done something wrong. I had a fat lip; did Marc Wilkey have any visible scars from the fight? My mom saw me moping around, and I told her what my dad had said.

"Oh, that man! Nothing's ever good enough for him. Lead with your left, give me a break!"

"That's a great credit," Sam said now. "How come you didn't tell me before?"

"I don't know. I thought it would look funny on the résumé, me playing a girl's part."

"We'll make it look right. Boys are so weird about anything that they think makes them look effeminate."

"What's effeminate?" I asked.

"Like a girl," Sam and Frog said in unison.

The other thing Frog thought to put on my résumé was a special skill: "He does great fart imitations."

"Anyone can do that," Sam said.

"Yeah, but can they do farts by the foods that cause them?" Frog asked.

"Like . . ."

"Bananas." I brought my arm up to my lips and did a loud banana fart.

"Three-bean salad," Frog requested. I complied with a machine-gun-style fart sound, completely different from bananas. Sam and Frog were both laughing.

"Give me another one," I said.

"Raisin bran," Sam said. I did a really long, low-volume, gassy one, sending us all into hysterical laughter. Sam and Frog threw in a few fart tones of their own. We went on like this for about half an hour.

Sam figured out a way to put my special skill on the résumé in a manner that wouldn't disgust all the casting directors in Hollywood.

My résumé was complete. Here's how it looked:

TYLER STEWART

Ht: 4' 10"   Hair: Blond
Wt: 98 lbs.   Eyes: Green

THEATER

Play	Role	Theater
Rumpelstiltskin	Rumpelstiltskin	Adlai Stevenson Center for the Arts
Cinderella (comedy version)	Cinderella	YMCA

FILM

Film	Role	
Surfer Dude*	Surfer	Lead
Boiled Lobster *	Lobster	Lead
Amnesia Man*	Man	Lead
Crazy Legs*	Guy	Lead
Duck out of Water *	Duck	Lead

PRINT

OshKosh B'Gosh clothing ad   Child in Overalls

TRAINING

Thelma Bennett

SPECIAL SKILLS

Musical: piano, singing
Unique imitations

*(short)

Pete was impressed that evening when I came home with my head shot and résumé. We were sitting at the dining room table drinking lemonades. Pete's apartment still hadn't cooled down from another blazing hot L.A. August day.

My head shot may not have looked exactly like the professional photos—all glossy with the name of the actor printed under the picture—but it was pretty close. The size of the head shot was the standard eight-by-ten, and the photo of me laughing that Kari had picked out looked great. On the back of the photo Sam had attached the résumé. Pete read it over. "Unique imitations?" he said. I gave him a quick demonstration. He chuckled, but I could tell he had something on his mind he wanted to talk about.

"Your dad called me today."

I started breathing a little harder. "What did he want?" I asked.

"He's worried about this audition. He just wanted to make sure I'd be there to look out for you." Pete paused. I knew there was something more to this. "He asked me if there was any real possibility of you getting a part on the show."

"What did you say?"

"I told him the truth: that there's gonna be a lot of boys with plenty of TV experience auditioning but that you're a funny kid, and you have a lot of natural talent, and if you give a good audition and seem right for the part, well then, you never know."

"You think I'm funny?"

"Yeah, and I think you could do this part."

That made me feel great. Pete wasn't one for handing out compliments unless he really meant it. Still, I felt there was something more to his conversation with my dad that he wasn't telling me.

14

On Mondays they routinely taped the exterior scenes for that week's episode. This usually meant going onto the Universal back lot, where there was a residential neighborhood filled with houses without interiors, called fronts, and taping stuff like the kids walking home or Jerry Stone pulling into the driveway and being greeted by Kari or one or more of the kids. Sometimes he'd step out of the car only to be smacked in the head by a Frisbee or something.

Pete and I got into a golf cart by the production bungalow and rode to the Parkers' street on the back lot. The cameramen, grips, costume and makeup people, P.A.s, sound people, etc. were all there. They had set up special lights and screens, almost in the same way Sam had done the day before, only this was on a much larger scale.

Since this was the Halloween episode, they were not only going to have to tape some scenes in the morning, but also come back in the evening and tape the night scenes of the kids trick-or-treating through the neighborhood. This meant a long, hard day for everyone, and it was even tougher because of the Screen Actors Guild rules about how long child actors can work. In addition to all this, today was the first day that the show's executive producers were going to audition kids for the new part of the problem boy.

In the scene they were taping, Grace is begging Marisol to take her to some fabulous Halloween party. Finally Marisol tells her, "I'd like to but I just don't have the authority." Grace snaps.

"Authority? Yeah, well, who gave you the authority to be a selfish pig!" and then runs into the house.

That scene consisted of about six lines but took over an hour to tape because Gretchen Harris's mother didn't like the idea of her daughter calling her TV-show sister a selfish pig. She seemed to think it would be bad for Gretchen's girl-next-door image. So while everyone sat around drinking coffee and eating Krispy Kremes, Baxter Rhodes and the network execs explained to Mrs. Harris that Grace calling Marisol a selfish pig was an essential part of the episode. In the end she'd say she was sorry, after a good talking-to from Colby Parker about the power of words and how they can hurt. Mrs. Harris was not convinced: "Why can't she just say 'You're being unfair' instead? I mean, she *is* being unfair. She should invite her to the dance."

Baxter Rhodes looked like he wanted to throw Mrs. Harris across the back lot and into the *Jaws* lagoon of the Universal tram tour. Instead he said, "Don't you see, this will give Gretchen an opportunity to show her acting depth. If you're concerned about her image after she leaves the show, this can only broaden her marketability." That seemed to strike the right note with Mrs. Harris, and they finally were able to shoot the scene.

Bonnie came by and asked if we wanted to go on a lunch run with her. Today's choice was the Daily Grill.

Sam and I sought Pete and Kari out to tell them where we were going. We found them together, talking. Pete looked serious but seemed to lighten up—almost too much—when he saw us. "Well, what do you think, Tyler? Is this what you were expecting a TV show would be like?"

"Not exactly," I said. "But I like it. It's fun and there's always something happening."

"Pete and I were talking about going to the TV museum or maybe the Griffith Observatory this weekend," Kari said.

"Just the two of you, or are we invited?" Sam said in her classic wisecracking voice. Pete and Kari gave each other a quick look, and then Pete said, "We thought it might be fun for all of us."

"Sure," said Sam. "We're going with Bonnie to pick up lunch."

Later, as we waited for the food at the Daily Grill, Sam said, "That was weird."

"What?"

"My mom and your uncle. They acted so weird when we came up to them. Like they were talking about something they didn't want us to know about. Maybe they really are going to start dating."

I had a different thought: that the conversation Pete and Kari were having had something to do with my audition. I still felt there was more to the conversation Pete had had with my dad the day before that he wasn't telling me.

When I told all this to Sam she said, "Could be, but I

also think there's something else going on between those two. Last night my mom said how great it was that you were here, because she might never have known what a great person Pete was if you hadn't shown up, become friends with me, and blah blah blah."

My cell phone started ringing. It was my mom, of course.

"Hi, Mom."

"Hi, honey. How are you? Has Pete talked to you about your audition?"

"Only that he's pretty sure he can get me one."

"Is that all he said?"

"Well, yeah. What's going on?"

"First of all, I know you're going to be great, but re-member what I said about not having your hopes up too high. Honey, I talked to your . . ." Her voice was breaking up. All I could make out were a few words in between the static. Words like "television" and "so angry" and "your father," and while she's breaking up I'm saying, "What? I can't hear you. Mom? Mom?" Then there was nothing. The phone rang again, and we went through a second series of unconnected words and phrase snip-pets: "don't worry about" *static static* "of him" *static static* "your best," and me saying, "I can't hear what you're saying. I'll call you when I get back to the studio. Bye."

What was going on? Did my dad want me to cut short my L.A. vacation and come stay with him for the next week? My mom thought I'd told my dad that I wouldn't be spending my days at the YMCA playing

Ping-Pong and making birdcages out of Popsicle sticks. Could she have unknowingly spilled the beans? I figured I was going to have to pay for that omission sooner or later but was hoping I could put it off until after I'd secured a role on *Kids*. I just couldn't figure it out. I knew, though, whatever it was, it wasn't going to be good.

When we got back to the production office, Sam ducked into the editing room, saying she'd catch up to me later. Bonnie and I toted the Daily Grill assortment of salads, pasta dishes, sandwiches, and turkey meat loaf for Pete, upstairs. I was anxious to get to a real phone and call my mom, but as we entered the writers' floor I was greeted by a startling sight: at least twenty-five boys about my age, all standing around with scripts in their hands, mumbling to themselves or to the adults chaperoning them. This was it. The auditions for the new kid in the house had begun.

15

We had just set the bags of food down in the writers' room when Pete came rushing over to me.

"Tyler, I need to talk to you." Pete didn't even stop to collect his lunch as he headed out the door and into his office. My mind was spinning. This must have to do with the phone call from my mom. Had she called Pete while we were bringing the food back to the studio?

"Sit down," Pete said.

Here it comes, I thought, *a plane ticket to New York.*

"You have an audition at two-thirty." He then pulled a few pieces of paper from the top of his desk. "Here's the scene you'll be reading."

My heartbeat seemed to immediately double. I couldn't wait to tell Sam. Then I remembered my mom's phone call, and my breathing became slightly labored. I wanted to call my mom and find out what was behind her mysterious phone call or ask Pete what it was that she might have been trying to tell me, but something told me to just concentrate on my audition and worry about everything else later.

Sam was sitting with Ed Conklin, the show's editor, who was making cuts and selecting the best shots to be used in the show they had taped last week. I was once again impressed with Sam's ability to learn just about anything she wanted to.

Sam looked over to the doorway I was hovering in. "What's up?"

"I have an audition at two-thirty."

"Awesome!" She immediately got up. "Thanks, Ed. I have to go help Tyler get his act together. Later." Ed just sort of grunted, never looking up from the screen.

Sam and I and the script pages made our way into Kari's dressing room. The first thing I did was tell her about my mom's strange call. I hadn't wanted to say anything while Bonnie was around.

"My advice is to not think about it until after you audition. Maybe it's nothing. Maybe your mom just didn't like it that your dad called Pete and told him what to do, and then maybe they had a big old fight and she just doesn't want you to worry about it."

"Maybe I should call her now?"

"No. 'Cause maybe I'm wrong. And besides, if it was really important, Pete would have said something, right?" I wasn't so sure but said "right" anyway.

"Let's run through your lines."

We sat together on Kari's couch. The audition scene was between my character, whose name was Ben, and Tom Parker. Like I said before, this new kid in the house was trouble. He'd been in more foster homes than anyone could count. The scene took place on the Parkers' patio in the evening. I could tell from Tom's first line that Ben must have done some awful things earlier in the show.

On paper it looked like this:

<u>EXT. PARKERS' PATIO—NIGHT</u>
TOM AND BEN ARE SITTING IN PATIO
CHAIRS.

TOM
Do you always try to make
trouble on your first day in a
new place?

BEN
What do you mean?

TOM
I've got two kids upstairs in
tears, another wants to move out,
and one more that wants to break
your arm.

BEN
(IMPASSIVELY) I really don't
care. I didn't do anything.

TOM
Yeah, you and Attila the Hun.

BEN
Ha ha! Just give me the rules.
This is usually where I get the
"rules of house" speech.

                    TOM

No. I don't think so. You're not
ready for the rules.

BEN IS SLIGHTLY TAKEN ABACK BUT
THEN GETS A SMIRK ON HIS FACE.

                    BEN

(SMART-ALECKY) Oh, I know. You
want to go out to the driveway
and play basketball with me.

                    TOM

No. I don't think so. You're not
ready for basketball in the
driveway.

                    BEN

(CONFUSED) So what am I ready for?

                    TOM

(RISING) Bed.

That was it. That was the scene that was going to get
me the part of the newest kid on *Kids in the House*. Of
course, first I had to do a great audition, which I guess I
wasn't on my way to doing, because midway through
our reading the scene Sam stopped and said, "You're
doing it too wimpy. Try it again, but first think of some

kid you know that acts all tough and above it all." I immediately thought of Marc Wilkey. This time when I said Ben's lines I tried to have them come out of my mouth in a way that they may have come out of Marc Wilkey's. All I wanted to do was impress everyone with how tough I was.

"Great!" Sam said. "But you're not quite there. It needs something else. It needs some pain. Not obvious pain, like you just got drilled by the dentist without novocaine, but deep-down pain that comes from being treated really bad by someone or losing someone you really care about."

"I don't think I've ever felt that way."

"How about when your parents got divorced?"

I thought about it. The truth was that when my dad first left, I was, in a strange way, relieved. I figured he wouldn't be telling me I was doing things the wrong way and going "earth to Tyler, earth to Tyler" all the time. But about a month after he'd moved out, a strange thing happened. I was in my room listening to a Cubs game when Sammy Sosa hit a home run in the bottom of the ninth to win it. I charged downstairs to tell my dad, and of course he wasn't there, and then I remembered: *He's not here, he's in New York.* I just stood there looking at the empty green leather chair where he'd normally be and was taken over by this incredibly sad feeling. I told this to Sam, who said that was what I should think about right before the scene begins. I did just that, and when we started the scene, I filled myself with Marc

Wilkey attitude, and before I knew it we had read through the entire scene.

"That was awesome!" Sam declared. "Now just do exactly the same thing when you go in for your audition."

We went back to the production offices. I got my picture and résumé out of a drawer in Pete's desk, where I'd stashed it earlier. Sam and I then waited with all the other boys and their parents outside the room where they were holding the auditions. One of the mothers was on a cell phone, and in a voice loud enough for the guard at the front gate to hear said, "Tomorrow at ten-thirty on the Radford lot . . . he'll be there."

I looked at Sam. "She's trying to psych out everyone else here," she said. "It's cutthroat with some of these parents. Just ignore her."

It was around two-forty-five when a woman came out of the audition room and said, "Tyler Stewart?"

"Good luck," Sam said. "Just do it the way you did before. You'll be great."

There were about half a dozen people in the room. There was Pete and Baxter Rhodes and several other high-end writers. A short, round woman in a business suit walked up to me. Glasses hung around her neck. She was no bigger than I was. "Hello, I'm Jan Gotlieb, the casting director."

"Hello, I'm Tyler Stewart, the actor." I hadn't intended to be funny, but everyone in the room suddenly broke into laughter.

"This is Pete's nephew," Baxter Rhodes said.

"So don't hold it against him," chimed in one of the other writers.

Jan pointed to my picture and résumé. "I'll take that."

I handed it to her. She lifted her glasses to her face. "Tell me about these films you put down here."

"They're on the Internet. I made them with a friend of mine."

"That's very creative. And I see you've done some print work. When did you do that?"

"When I was younger," I said nervously.

Jan could spot an exaggeration with just a glance. It was as if someone had taken a yellow marker and highlighted anything on a résumé that looked suspicious, which in my case was almost everything. Jan's eyes peered at me from over her glasses. "How young?" she asked. I shot a look over to Pete, who gave me a little "go ahead, tell the truth" nod.

"Two years."

"Two years ago?"

"No, two years old . . . but I was big for my age." Again the room burst into laughter. Baxter Rhodes was now standing behind Jan, looking at my résumé. "Hey, Tyler, what are these unique imitations that you do?" The last thing I wanted to say to this group of adults was that I was an expert in fart mimicry, but I was on the spot and couldn't think of anything else to say. "I do fart imitations," I said. More laughter. "On my arm," I added. More laughter. "Can you do chili beans with onions?" Baxter asked.

"Yes."

"Go ahead."

"Right now?"

"Sure."

I put my lips to my forearm and let out a big long chili-beans-with-onions fart noise. Everyone laughed. Now I was in on the joke and felt a lot better. I rolled off a couple of other fart requests, wondering what the kids and their parents just outside the room were thinking. I now felt totally comfortable with Jan and Baxter and everyone else in the room.

"All right, let's read the scene," Jan said.

It was Pete who read the part of Tom Parker, which made me even more comfortable.

I remembered everything that Sam had told me to remember. Before we started, I took a moment to recall how I felt that day when I realized my dad was really gone. Then, as soon as Jan said "Begin," I let Marc Wilkey's attitude take over my body. I didn't think about anyone in the room or what they might be thinking. I just reacted to whatever Pete said, trying to impress him with how tough I was.

When we finished, Jan said, "Good. Very good. Thank you, Tyler."

"That was great, Tyler. Thanks," Baxter said.

Pete gave me a nod and said, "Nice work. Don't go too far away."

I walked out the door and over to Sam. "How did it go?" she said. "I heard laughter. What was that about?"

"I think they liked me. Baxter Rhodes said I did great."

"And the laughs?"

"Special-skills demonstration."

"Get out of here."

"It's true." We noticed that the other boys and their mothers and agents were looking at us, not exactly enjoying our enthusiasm, so we slipped into Pete's office.

"What about the reading? Did you remember to do it like I said?"

"Exactly like you said, and I got to read it with Pete."

"Awesome! I'll bet you get a callback." As soon as Sam said "callback," a jolt of apprehension went through my body. "I've got to call my mom back," I said.

"Oh, yeah. I forgot about that too. You better do that." Sam headed for the door. "I'll be back later. Don't worry, everything will be cool."

Sam closed the door behind her while I pulled the piece of paper out of my wallet that had my mom's hotel phone number on it, as well as other "emergency" numbers.

The hotel put me through to my mom's room. Raphael answered.

"Hi, Raphael. It's Tyler. Is my mom—"

"Tyler! How did you do in your audition? Did you remember to give them your teeth?"

"Yeah, I remembered. It went really well. Can I talk to my mom?"

"Sure, sure. She's coming out of the bathroom right now. Good work, kid."

In the background I could hear my mom say, "Is that

Tyler?" and Raphael saying, "*Si, si,* yes, your boy did great."

My mom's voice came on the line: "I hear you did great at your audition. Is that true?"

"Yeah, I think they liked me a lot." I then gave her a full recap of my audition, special-skills demonstration and all.

"I am so proud of you, no matter what happens from here. I am sure that Pete has told you there are so many things that are out of your control . . ."

"I know, Mom."

"And this thing with your father. I don't want you to worry about that at all. I'll take care of him."

"What thing? I couldn't hear you earlier."

"Pete hasn't told you?"

"He just said that Dad wanted to make sure that he was in the room when I auditioned."

"Oh, your father! He's just impossible. He has to control everything; no room for anyone else's feelings or needs."

"What did he say?"

"Your father told Pete that it was all right for you to have the experience of auditioning for the show and seeing what really went on in the TV business. But on the chance that you might get cast, there was no way that he would ever allow you to work on 'that television show,' as he put it."

"But, Mom—"

"Now, don't you worry, honey. I told him that there is

no way that I would allow *him* to interfere with your success in this or anything else."

"What did Pete say?"

"Well, Pete called me, and I told him that I'd handle your father and that he should just encourage you to do your best."

I was happy to know that my mom wouldn't side with my dad to protect me from the evils of Tinseltown. Sometimes my dad's "I'm right and know what's best for everyone" attitude is a sure way to get my mom to take the opposite point of view.

"Is that it?"

"Well, he did threaten to fly out to Los Angeles if necessary, but I'm sure it won't come to that."

My dad flying out to Los Angeles was about the worse thing that could happen. I was extremely lucky that he hadn't learned that I'd not been spending my days at the YMCA. He'd certainly be angry with me if he found *that* out. He'd be sure to go right up to the executive producers and network representatives and tell them his opinion of Hollywood. I'd heard it often enough: "It's a horrible place. They use you until they can't use you anymore. Everybody's so phony. And for a child it's the worst. They fill you with ego and false praise, alienate you from your family, and then, when you're not so cute anymore, well, then you're on your own."

No, I didn't want my dad flying out to L.A. If he did, any chance of my becoming a kid in the house would vanish, no matter what my mom said.

16

"**You'll** never get lunch for anyone in this town again" was Sam's wry comment when I'd told her about my dad's threat. We were back on the Parkers' street getting ready to do the nighttime preshoots for the Halloween episode. Eddie McNamara overheard me complaining to Sam about my dad. "Your dad's nothing compared to mine," he grunted. "If I wasn't about to turn eighteen, I'd be suing him to get control over my career and money. Like he's done anything for me." The assistant director called to Eddie that they were ready to shoot the next scene. As he walked away, Sam whispered, "I think it's a good idea that if your dad does come to L.A., you keep him away from Eddie."

Pete walked up to us. I hadn't seen him since the audition. They'd been looking at other potential Bens all afternoon.

"They want to see you again," Pete said. "Nice going."

"All right! You got a callback!" Sam said gleefully.

I just stood there, unable to breathe.

"Hey, what's wrong? Aren't you happy?"

"You okay, Tyler?" Pete asked, starting to get concerned.

I wheezed out a "can't breathe." In the rush and excitement and distress of everything that was happening,

I'd forgotten to take my asthma medication. Now I was having a full-on asthma attack.

You know that saying "It's as easy as breathing"? Well, whoever said that never suffered from asthma. Your chest feels like it has a rock in it, and though you're gasping in air, none of it seems to be getting through to your lungs. My asthma medications, including my inhaler, which helped to keep my airways free and open, were sitting on Pete's kitchen counter.

To make things even worse the heat went up to about 120 degrees when Pete, Sam, and I climbed into Pete's Corolla.

Sam was with me in the backseat, looking as white as I probably looked. "Shouldn't he be breathing into a paper bag or something?" she asked Pete.

"It doesn't really help. They'll give him a shot in the emergency room and then he should be okay." I nodded my agreement and wheezed out a "Right."

"Hang in there, pal, we'll be there in a few minutes." Pete sped through traffic, dodging cars, honking his horn, and gunning it through intersections whenever the light was turning from yellow to red.

Before long we pulled up in front of the emergency entrance at the hospital. My breathing hadn't improved much. It was still like trying to suck a milk shake through a straw that's blocked up with a blueberry or something. We scrambled through the door and up to the admissions desk. If my mom had been with me, she would have been screaming from the time we entered the emergency room that her son couldn't breathe and needed to be attended to immediately. They would have quickly gotten to me just to shut her up. With Pete in charge it took a bit longer, but he was still pretty good at making sure I got seen right away. I was taken into a curtained-off area where they gave me some oxygen and the shot I needed to get me back to normal. I had been wheezing and gasping for almost twenty minutes, and I can't tell you how wonderful it felt to get a full breath of air into my lungs.

Pete and Sam were as relieved as I was. "You had me freaked," Sam said as we walked out of the hospital and back to Pete's car. "I thought you were going to check out on us."

Pete was more serious. "Sam, I'm going to drop you off at the studio and then take Tyler home."

"I'm okay now," I said.

"No, I think it's better if you go home."

"To Chicago?" I was still a little light-headed from no air and then getting all that oxygen.

"To my place."

"You definitely need a hiatus," Sam threw in.

"Okay," I said, exhausted from the day's events. "I'll be in my trailer."

It was around eight P.M. when we got back to Pete's apartment. Pete went to his beverage-only refrigerator and pulled out a couple of cherry colas. He handed one to me and then picked up the phone. "I'm going to call your mom," he said.

I nodded. I knew we had to do this, but I also knew it

would send my mom into a frenzy. Here she was in Cancún taking a stress-reducing vacation from motherly du-
ties with her goofy new boyfriend, and then I have to go
and have a giant asthma attack.

It took a while for the hotel people to track down my
mom. I could picture her at some beachside cabana, sipping umbrella drinks with Raphael, when a hotel waiter
would walk up to her and say, *"Mrs. Stewart?"* From that
simple "Mrs. Stewart?" my mom would immediately
know that something was wrong. *"What is it? What's
happened?"* she'd say anxiously.

"A telephone call for you."

"Oh my God. Something's happened to Tyler," she'd
start screaming, possibly on her way to hysteria.

Another voice, this time Raphael's, would come in:
*"Relax, Laura, it's probably a good thing. Your boy is
maybe a TV star."*

When my mom finally came on the line, Pete, not
wanting her to get too freaked, did a classic downplay of
my recent trauma: "Hey, Lor, first of all, Tyler is fine. . . .
Well, he had a little asthma problem. . . . No, no, not too
serious, his breathing was just a little heavy. . . . Well, he,
um, left it here in my apartment. . . . I know, it's totally
my fault. It won't happen again. I promise. . . . Well, I did
take him to the hospital . . . No, no, it was just a cautionary measure. . . . Lor, he's fine, really. . . . They gave him a
shot just to be safe, you know. . . . No, that's not necessary. You finish your vacation. He's fine. Oh, and he did a
great audition today, did he tell you? . . . Yeah. Okay, here
he is." Pete handed me the phone.

"Hi, Mom."

"Are you all right, honey?"

"I'm fine, Mom. It wasn't bad at all. I knew I was all right, but Pete made me go to the hospital anyway." Pete made an "okay" sign from across the room.

"Tyler, you know you're supposed to keep your inhaler with you all the time."

"I know, Mom. I forgot. I'm sorry."

"I just worry so much about you."

"I won't forget again. Really. Guess what, Mom, I got a callback," I said excitedly.

"You did? Oh, that's wonderful, honey! Do you want me there with you?"

I thought about it for a second. I didn't really have a problem with my mom being there for the callback, not like I might if my dad was there, but I liked the way things were going with Pete and Sam helping me. I didn't want to mess it up by making too much of it. Plus if my mom was there, then Raphael would be there, saying stuff like "Don't forget to give them your teeth."

"No," I said. "Maybe if things go well at the callback."

"All right. Well, just do your best. I know you will, and don't forget to have your inhaler with you. Always. I don't know what I'd do if something happened to you."

I handed the phone back to Pete. He mostly just said "Right, right" for the next few minutes. After he'd hung up, I asked him what else my mom had said.

"She just wanted to make sure I kept a closer eye on you." I felt there must have been more to it, what with all the "right, right"s, but decided to let it go.

He then said, "I didn't see any point in getting your mom all upset about our little trip to the hospital."

"Thanks," I said.

"But she's right, I do need to keep a closer eye on you. . . . Hey, you rocked this afternoon."

"Really?"

"Really. You were great. Everyone loved you, that's why they're calling you back."

"When? Tomorrow?"

"No. Tomorrow's a tape night and Jerry's gonna be busy all day. We'll do it on Wednesday after the table-read."

"I have to audition with Jerry Stone?" I asked nervously.

"Well, he is an executive producer and star of the show. You've got a problem with that?"

Great. Jerry Stone, who I'd crashed into when my feet got tangled in camera cables; Jerry Stone, whose scene I'd interrupted when my cell phone went off; Jerry Stone, who I'd totally stepped in it with by mentioning his hair transplant. Jerry Stone would be reading the scene with me at my callback.

"No problem," I said.

"What do you say we turn on *SportsCenter* and see how the Cubs did today?"

"Sure."

As we sat on the sofa watching the ESPN guys running through the day's scores, all my exhausted brain could think about was the tarot reading that Kari had given me a few days before and the stern-looking King of Swords—*a man who could pose a strong obstacle for you.* Was the King of Swords my dad? Was it Jerry Stone? Both?

Before the ESPN guys got to the Cubs game, I was asleep.

17

By the time I'd gotten dressed the next morning, Pete had placed TYLER'S MEDICATION and DON'T FORGET INHALER Post-its on his bulletin board and refrigerator and, just to be safe, on the front door. I had no desire to make a repeat trip to the hospital, so at this point there was very little chance of my forgetting. In fact, the first thing I'd done that morning was take my medication and put my inhaler in my cargo shorts. Still, I think it made Pete feel safer to have all those reminder notes up and to ask me ten times if I had my inhaler with me.

That night they would be taping the Halloween episode in front of a live audience. The actors would be rehearsing all day. The writers, barring any emergency problems on the set, would be doing a quick pass over the script that would be table-read the next day. On that same day, along with the other boys who'd gotten called back for the role of Ben, I'd be reading with Jerry Stone. If I did well—and it was a big if—I could be the next kid in the house. I could be in living rooms across America every Thursday night at eight P.M. I'd be on the show for a few years, my face popping out of teen-magazine covers in supermarkets. Beyond that were movies and reruns of *Kids* that could last forever. That was if my dad didn't ruin everything by refusing to let me be on the show.

There was no way stardom was going to turn me into a spoiled kid celebrity like Eddie McNamara or Gretchen Harris or a spoiled adult celebrity like Jerry Stone—Jerry Stone, who I was sure hated me, and who, like my dad, had the power to ruin everything.

Before going up to Pete's office, we went over to the set to find Sam and Kari and grab some fruit and pastries off the craft service table. I was surprised to see a lot of people come up and ask how I was doing. I guess word had gotten around the set from the night before. Even Faith Remo, who I had not had two words with since Sam introduced us on my first night in town, asked if I was feeling better. I got a little starstruck looking into Faith's deep brown eyes, which genuinely seemed concerned for my well-being. As she walked away, Sam came up and in a singsong voice said, "I think someone's in love."

"No way," I said, sorry that Sam had caught me gawking at Faith.

"Wow, I never realized that asthma was such a chick magnet," Pete joked.

"You two are a terrible combination," Kari, who had just joined us, said to Pete and Sam.

"You can take it, right?" Sam said to me.

"Yeah, I can take it," and then in a voice like Arnold Schwarzenegger's I said, "And I can dish it out, too. Slap! Slap! Slap!" Sam acted as though my fake swings at her were connecting like prizefighter blows and she fell to the ground. As she did, the actors were called to their places to start rehearsal.

"Well, I'm glad nothing serious happened to you," Kari said.

"Yeah, me too," I said.

Pete then said, "All right, I have to get to work. You got your inhale—"

"I've got it," I cut in, holding up my inhaler for Pete to see.

"Good. Okay, well, don't wander off without telling me."

"Okay," I said.

Sam filled a paper plate with fruit while I munched on the bear claw I had grabbed a few minutes earlier. "Does your mom know about my callback tomorrow?" I asked. I knew by now that even though Kari was a star of the show, she didn't have any real power in making decisions about who did or who did not get cast. Not like Jerry Stone, who was a star and also an executive producer. Still, it would be nice to have her in my corner.

"She knows," Sam said. "She just doesn't want to make too big a deal about it."

"Why? Does she think I'll be too disappointed if I don't get it?"

"Maybe that, too. Mainly she's just superstitious and doesn't want to jinx it for you."

I totally got it. I remember once hearing the Cubs announcer say that if someone was pitching a no-hitter, none of the other players or coaches on the team would say anything about it, for fear of jinxing him.

I was pretty keyed up about the callback audition. I wished it could be have been that day instead of the next. I grabbed a basketball from Pete's office, and Sam and I walked over to a hoop between soundstages. We were on our second game of H-O-R-S-E when my cell phone went off.

"Hi, Mom," I automatically said.

"Try again," the male voice on the other end of the line said.

"Dad?"

"What are you doing?"

I suddenly remembered that in my dad's brain I was at the YMCA.

"Just shooting baskets," I said, not having to lie.

I sat down in the shadow of the basket, Sam pulling up a piece of concrete next to me.

"Great. Listen, son, your mother says Pete took you to the hospital last night. You all right?"

"Yeah, I'm fine, Dad. It was more of a cautionary measure," I said, using Pete's downplay from the night before.

I was starting to feel guilty about my omissions and downplays. The longer you wait to be completely honest about something, the harder it becomes to say it.

"Are you back in New York?" I asked, trying to move the subject away from me.

"Got back last night. I heard you did well at your audition."

"Yeah, they want to see me again tomorrow."

"Son, I want you to do well, of course I do, but I want you to be careful that you don't get your hopes up too high." I wasn't sure if he meant too high because he didn't think I'd get the part, or too high because he'd never let me *do* the part.

I was a little scared to hear the answer, but I asked him anyway. "Dad, if I get this part, you'll let me do it, right?"

"Tyler, it's very complicated. It would be an enormous decision that your mother and I would have to make. The two of you would have to move from Chicago to L.A.; all of our lives would change dramatically. Especially yours. Sometimes the things we want are not always what's best for us."

Great, I thought, *he's pulling out the old wants-versus-needs lecture.*

"Can't what I want also be what's best for me?"

"Let's just take this one step at a time. We'll talk again after your audition tomorrow."

"Okay."

"I love you, son."

"Bye, Dad."

"What's the matter?" Sam asked as I slipped my cell phone back into my cargo shorts.

"He didn't even wish me good luck."

"Come on," Sam said. "I know something that will cheer you up."

Sam and I spent most of the afternoon in Pete's office playing computer games. I think she was trying to distract me from thinking about the next day's audition with Jerry Stone and the possibility of my dad putting the kibosh on the whole thing. We were in the middle of a game of Enemies from Hell when I said to Sam, "Shouldn't I be practicing for tomorrow?"

"Nah," she said without talking her eyes off the screen, continuing to blast away at gargoyles. "It's best not to overrehearse. You don't want to lose your spontaneity. I think that's your best quality." She had helped me get this far, so I figured she must be right and we continued to play the game.

At around five we had dinner with Pete and Kari, and just about everyone else involved with the show, in one of the studio dining halls. The setup was nothing fancy: long folding tables like you might see in any school cafeteria, in a room with unadorned white walls and a brown linoleum floor. The food, however, was catered by some four-star restaurant that I can't remember the name of. The longer I stayed in Hollywood, the more it seemed everything was about the food.

Jerry Stone was sitting not far from us with a woman who I assumed was his girlfriend, since Frog had informed me that he wasn't married. Frog, by the way, was psyched that I'd gotten a callback and especially pleased that the résumé information he'd supplied had been helpful.

Did Jerry know I would be auditioning with him the next day? Did he care? I was probably the last kid in the world that he'd want to let into the Parker household.

Kari was still not mentioning my audition, and by now I was starting to feel a little superstitious myself. So we talked about everything *but* my audition, mostly what we were going to do over the weekend.

The taping of the Halloween episode went incredibly well. There was a new stand-up comedian that week to warm up the studio audience and keep their energy up between scenes. This guy not only told jokes and explained stuff about the show, but juggled, did impressions, got people from the audience on their feet singing songs and dancing, and gave pop quizzes about the show's history, rewarding the winners with *Kids* T-shirts, mugs, and hats.

Sam and I went back and forth between sitting in the audience and standing on the floor. I was careful this time not to get in the way of any cameras, cables, or Jerry Stone. My cell phone was turned off.

At one point, in between scenes and trips to the craft service table, Sam turned to me and said, "Come on, let's have some fun."

In addition to the actors, writers, technicians, network and studio executives, and a smattering of relatives and friends of the show's stars and producers who had access to the privileged concrete of the studio floor, there were . . . agents. They seemed to bunch together behind everyone else, never getting in the way but making their presence clearly known, as if to say *I'm your agent. I'm here. I support you. My agency supports you* to their clients involved in the show or, in the case of *Kids*, the parents of the child stars.

We walked up to one of the men in an agent cluster. "Hey, Walter," Sam said.

"Samantha, how are you?"

"Walter works for ICM, that's my mom's agency." I

just nodded. "This is Tyler. His uncle is one of the writers. Pete Marcowitz."

"Uh-huh. Nice to meet you, Tyler."

"Hi."

Walter was turning back to the other agents when Sam said, "It looks like Tyler may be the next kid in the house." Walter stopped in midturn and swung back in our direction. The agents' conversation on the other side of him trickled off. "Really?" Walter said.

"Yeah, everyone raved about his audition the other day, and tomorrow he has a callback with Jerry."

"Who represents you?" Walter asked casually.

"I do?" I said, not exactly knowing what he meant.

"Do you have an agent?"

"Oh, not yet."

Like a magician, he suddenly had a card in the palm of his hand as he pulled me away from the pack of agents. He handed me his card and said, "Have your parents give me a call tomorrow. If everything works out, our agency can do a lot for you and your family."

Within the next half hour at least four more agents from the pack had given me their cards and told me to have my parents call them.

"That was weird," I said when Sam and I were once again alone.

"That's just a taste of what it will be like if you get on the show. Every agent in town will be calling your parents, trying to sign you."

I was feeling a lot of different stuff all at once. I was flattered that all these agents might want to sign me.

On the other hand, none of them had seen a thing I'd ever done. It was all based on what Sam had said about my callback audition the following day.

"Well, you don't have to worry about it anyway. Your dad's a lawyer, so he can make your deals for you. Hey, are you okay? You're not going to stop breathing again, are you?"

"I'm fine," I said as the studio bell rang to make everyone be quiet. But I wasn't really fine. It had suddenly hit me that if I got the part, my life really would be totally different. And for the first time I wasn't sure that would be such a great thing.

Like the week before, at certain times there were lines that fell flat. That's when Pete and the other writers would huddle together and pitch new lines to Baxter Rhodes, who would decide what to use and then go over to Jerry or Kari or one of the kids and give them the new line. Sam and I tried to get in as close as we could whenever this would happen. The best person at coming up with new funny lines was Neal Peachy. Time after time throughout the night, Neal would pitch a line at Baxter, who would then say, "Let's try that," and the next minute the studio audience would be laughing hysterically. I was beginning to see why Neal got paid so much money. The most important time that they needed a good laugh line was at the end of a scene, what the writers called the blow. More than once that night, it was Pete who came up with new blows that had the house rocking with laughter. It was great to see him be that funny under all that pressure. Pete was cool.

The other person who had a fantastic show that night was Jerry Stone. The guy may have been a creep offstage, but once he was in front of the cameras, you couldn't take your eyes off him, whether he was doing one of his famous pratfalls or thoughtfully giving advice to one of the kids. During the curtain call the audience gave him a thunderous standing ovation. After the show Jerry went around shaking hands with the cast and crew, saying, "Great show! Great show!"

I just hoped his good mood would carry over to the next day.

18

The following morning was the table-read for the next episode. Later in the day I'd be reading with Jerry Stone. I had hoped he would still be soaring from his uproarious performance the night before. No such luck. Jerry was his normal, surly self, wearing dark glasses and slouching in his chair all through the table-read.

This week's episode would be the first of four involving Grace getting reconnected with her birth mom and eventually leaving the Parker household and the show. The episodes were slated to run during November sweeps, one of several periods each season when the networks vied for top ratings. The trades—*The Hollywood Reporter* and *Variety*—were already reporting that Gretchen Harris, who played Grace, was leaving the show. "Her publicist is telling everyone that Gretchen is leaving because of all the offers she's getting to do movies," Sam was saying as we waited for the table-read to begin, "but everyone here knows it's because no one can stand her or her mother anymore." Gretchen was sitting next to Faith Remo, whose character, Marisol, going on her first date was this week's B story, and who I had trouble taking my eyes off of whenever I saw her. Sam, of course, spotted me looking at Faith and couldn't pass up an opportunity to give me a hard time about it. "How's your girlfriend?" she needled.

"She's not my girlfriend."

"Do you lu-u-uv her?"

"Shut up."

"I'm just kidding. She's old enough to be your older sister, which I guess she will be if you get on the show."

All right, so I had a little crush on Faith. That was no reason for Sam to be pointing it out all the time.

The third, or C, story that week was about the little kids, George, Choon-Yei, and Razieh, going camping in the backyard.

Baxter Rhodes introduced this week's guest stars and director, who announced, "Interior, the Parkers' living room, day," and the table-read began.

Though the reading was going great—lots of laughs and not just from the writers—it was hard for me to think about anything but my callback audition later that day. My mom had phoned me before Pete and I had left for the studio to wish me luck and give me her "Just do your best; I love you no matter what" speech. In my e-mail that morning, Frog had told me to break a leg—using the correct show business lingo—and passed on some advice he'd gathered from famous actors:

"Just say the lines clearly and don't bump into the furniture."—Tallulah Bankhead

"Acting is merely the art of keeping a large group of people from coughing."—Sir Ralph Richardson

"The most important thing about acting is honesty. If you can fake that, you've got it made."—George Burns

There was nothing from my dad.

After the table-read several of the nonsuperstitious

119

actors came up to me and wished me good luck with the audition. Eddie McNamara said, "It's in the bag, kid," but I don't think he really cared. Faith Remo gave me a sincere "I hope you do well at your audition." I thanked her but was careful not to stare at her too long, not wanting to get another teasing from Sam. Kari was still acting like nothing special was going on, but by now I knew that meant that she really wanted me to ace the audition.

Sam and I walked back to the production office with Pete. The mob of kid actors and accompanying parents from the other day had been narrowed to about a dozen. Pete said I should go wait in his office and that there were audition pages, called sides, on his desk. He then went into the casting room.

I was happy to have Pete's office to duck into. "All right, let's read through it once," Sam said, closing the door. I had taken her advice and not overrehearsed, hoping to keep my reading fresh. "Just do everything you did last time."

We each were holding a copy of the audition side. "Take your time," she said. Once again I went through my ritual: first, thinking about the time I'd run downstairs to tell my dad about Sammy Sosa's home run, only to remember that he didn't live with us anymore; then, taking on Marc Wilkey's tough attitude, and finally, reading the scene with Sam and, as Thelma Bennett would say, simply reacting.

"Fantastic," Sam said when we'd finished. "Now I know you're kinda freaked that Jerry's going to read with you."

"Yeah, a little," I admitted.

"I thought about that and here's what I think you should do. If you find yourself starting to want to impress Jerry with your acting, tell yourself to impress him with how tough you are instead. Okay?"

"Yeah."

"That's something my mom does. She calls it substitution or channeling her fears or something like that, but it works whenever she gets nervous or distracted, especially in auditions."

"Your mom still has to audition?"

"It never ends. All right, now I think we should play Enemies from Hell."

About fifty minutes later, Pete came though the door and said, "Okay, you're on deck, pal." I suddenly got really nervous. "Just go in and have fun," he said casually. "I'll see you in there."

I took a deep breath. Actually it was a pretty shallow breath, so I pulled out my inhaler and gave myself a couple of quick bursts of Proventil.

"I'll wait for you in here," Sam said. "Remember, impress Jerry with how tough you are."

"Right."

I walked out of Pete's office and into the general waiting area. All the other kids and their parents were gone, with the exception of one man who undoubtedly was the father of the boy currently auditioning. He looked incredibly tense. I wondered if he gave his son lectures on the evils of Hollywood. Probably not. I wondered if he was always barking out instructions on how to do things better. Maybe. I wondered about my own dad and wasn't sure if I was disappointed or relieved that he hadn't contacted me that morning.

The door to the casting room swung open and a boy about my own age, maybe a little older, came out and was greeted by the man. "How did it go?" the father asked.

"Pretty good, I guess."

"What do you mean, you guess?" his father said harshly.

"I don't know. It was fine. Just leave me alone," the boy snapped, and then quickly walked away.

"Alan, come back here!" The father was now running after Alan, who had just kept walking.

That was weird, I thought. It was as if the mortgage on the house were riding on Alan's audition. I didn't have much more time to think about it because the casting-room door had once again opened, and I was being asked to come inside.

Now, in addition to Pete, Jan Gotlieb, Baxter Rhodes, and several of the other writers, there were a number of executives from the studio and network, or what everyone called suits. There was also a video camera set up at the back of the room.

There were two chairs at the front. One was empty and in the other sat Jerry Stone. Jan walked up to me and said, "Tyler, nice to see you again."

"Thanks" was all I could get out, my heart beating rapidly.

"Hi, Tyler," Baxter said. "Jerry, I think you've met Pete's nephew, Tyler."

"Who's Pete?"

"Pete Marcowitz, one of our writers."

Pete raised his hand to identify himself.

"Just kidding," Jerry said, but I wasn't so sure. He then turned to me and said, "It's the kid who likes magic." That threw me a little. The last time I'd talked to Jerry when I'd made the giant flub about his hair transplant, he'd said something about "making children disappear." Was this now his coded way of telling me he was still holding it against me?

"Have a seat," Jan said. I took my place next to Jerry. I couldn't look at him. "Okay, Tyler, you know the scene. You ready?"

"I just need a moment," I said. For some reason this caused some chuckles in the room. Jerry then said, "Oh, I see we have a *method actor* with us," which caused more laughs. I let that go and focused on the moment of realizing my dad was really gone. A feeling of sadness came over me, Then it was Marc Wilkey's image that came into my mind. Jan said, "Ready?"

"Yeah."

We started the scene. It was all much more serious with Jerry reading his own part. Early on I started thinking, *Jerry hates me, he thinks I stink*, but instead of trying harder to make him think I was a good actor, I did what Sam had suggested and tried harder to show him how tough I was. That was the main thing I thought about, whether it was my line or Jerry's, and I took Thelma's advice of *really* listening to him, so that many of my reactions surprised even me.

Jerry spoke the last line of the scene. There was a brief silence, broken by Jan saying, "Very good, Tyler. Thank you."

"Nice work, Tyler," Baxter said.

I looked around, not sure what came next. "You can go now," Jan said.

I looked at Pete, who gave me a nod and a smile, and then I left the room.

"Well?" Sam said when I walked back into Pete's office. I shrugged. "How did it feel?" she asked.

"Good. Really good."

"What were you expecting, that they'd just give you the part right then and there?"

"No." But that's exactly what I'd been thinking or at least hoping.

I then told her about Jerry's "magic" remark.

"Yeah, that sounds like Jerry, always letting people know that their fate lies in his hands. But that doesn't mean he won't want you on the show. He may be a jerk but he's also a perfectionist, so if you're good and right for the part, he'll give you his backing—and then never let you forget it."

"So now what?"

"You wait," Sam said, picking up Pete's basketball, "and I beat your butt at hoops."

Sam and Kari went home in the early evening. Pete was in the room with the other writers doing a rewrite of the script that had been table-read earlier that day. I went into Pete's office and phoned my

mom, telling her all about my callback audition with
Jerry.

"What did Pete say?"

"Just that I'd done great and that we'd have to wait
and see. They might still want to look at some other kids."

The fact that I hadn't told my dad about spending
my days at the studio instead of the YMCA was starting
to weigh heavily on me. I wanted to tell my mom but
was afraid that it might start a chain reaction ending
with my dad saying that I'd already been corrupted by
Tinseltown and he'd better get me out of there before I
turned up on the next *E! True Hollywood Story* about the
tragic lives of former child stars.

"How's Raphael?" I said instead.

"Oh, he's fine. Wants to drag me to some more ruins
tomorrow. Frankly, I've had enough of this vacation. I
can only relax so much. I've already read all the books I
brought with me. The only things they have in the gift
shop are romance novels. Are you sure you don't want
me to fly up there?"

"I guess if I get the part you'll have to, but Pete thinks
we should—"

"I know," my mom interrupted, "wait and see."

That night Pete and I ate submarine sandwiches and
watched the Cubs play the Dodgers on Pete's giant TV.
"You did great today, you know that?" Pete said during a
commercial.

"Yeah, I felt like I did good."

"I was really proud of you. You handled yourself well

in that room with all those suits and especially with Jerry. The guy can be a pain."

"So, do you think I'll get it?"

"I don't know. There were a lot of people with a lot of opinions in that room. And when the network gets involved, anything can happen. I'll tell you this, as far I'm concerned, you were the best of all the kids we've seen."

For some reason, Pete saying what he did made me feel all mushy inside, and before I knew what was happening, the truth popped out.

"My dad thinks I'm spending my days at the Y."

"What?" Pete asked, totally confused.

"I never told my dad that I'd be at the studio instead of the YMCA."

"Does your mom know?"

"She knows I'm at the studio, but she thinks I got Dad's permission."

"Whoa, pal, it looks like you got yourself in the soup."

"What should I do?"

"You've got to tell them. Let's call your mom now."

"Can't we wait till the morning?" I guess I wanted to hold on to the glowing feeling I still had from having done well at my audition. If everything was going to come crashing down on me, I wanted to put it off just a little longer. Maybe Pete sensed this, because he said, "All right, pal, we'll call her in the morning."

We turned our attention back to the game, but I couldn't help thinking about my own fate, when, in the ninth inning, the Cubs blew a three-run lead and went down to defeat.

19

My mom must have been in a Mexican jungle or a pyramid or both with Raphael the next morning; that's the only explanation I have for her not returning my call. I wasn't about to say anything to my dad until I talked to her, knowing that I needed her to buffer his fury. Not that she was going to be happy about what I had done.

When we arrived at the studio, there was no news about the part. Baxter Rhodes saw me and said, "You did great yesterday." But that was all. I got similar pats on the back from several of the other writers who had been in the room at my callback, but no "It's in the bag" from anyone.

I went online to see if my dad had sent me any e-mail. There was nothing. Sam walked into the room. "What's up?" she said.

"He doesn't even care if I did well or not."

"Who, Jerry?"

"No, my dad."

"Yeah, I hear you on that one."

I then told Sam about my confession to Pete and how I was waiting for my mom to call and how upset my dad would be when he found out I'd deceived him.

"Let's get out of here," Sam said boldly.

"What do you mean?"

"Let's go up to the theme park." The Universal Studios Theme Park was just a ten-minute walk up the hill from where our bungalow sat. "I'll tell my mom; you tell Pete and get some cash and we'll just go on rides all day."

"What about my mom?"

"You've got your phone with you, right?"

"Yeah."

"Then let's go."

We grabbed some snacks from the craft service table on the soundstage, got Bonnie to drive us up the hill in one of the carts, and just like that we were inside the theme park.

For the next few hours we went from ride to ride, doing repeats on Jurassic Park and Back to the Future. We watched the Wild, Wild, Wild West Stunt Show and checked out WaterWorld. We hadn't said a word about my audition or my dad or her dad or anything to do with *Kids in the House*. Then, just before the beginning of the Terminator 2 show Sam said, "If you get on the show and come back here next year, everyone will want your autograph."

"That would be cool," I said. But as the show began I thought: Would it be cool? What if one day I didn't feel like signing autographs and just wanted to go to a movie or a ball game and be left alone? Would I have to go in disguise? I pictured myself in dark glasses, a baseball cap lowered over my forehead, and my coat pulled up around my chin. I guess it was a small price to pay for all the fame and money I'd be getting.

As we walked back down the hill toward the bungalow, I asked Sam if her mom ever got tired of being a
celebrity.

"She loves it. You should see her with fans, she's
really pretty great. She's always thanking them, saying
that because of them she gets to do something she loves,
acting. And she means it. But she did have a stalker a
couple of years ago. She didn't love that too much."

"What happened?"

"Some guy started sending her flowers, perfume,
and even some pretty expensive jewelry. There would
always be creepy notes saying how beautiful she was
and how much he loved her and begging her for just one
date to show her what a normal, upstanding guy he
was. Up standing in our rose bushes, as it turned out.
The police took him away, and now he can't come
within two hundred yards of our house or my mom, no
matter where she is."

Pete had been assigned to write the next script and
was in his office working on it when we got back to the
bungalow. I asked him if my mom had called, in case she
had tried my cell phone while we were in the middle of
Back to the Future or something.

"Not yet," he said.

"Any word on the part?" Sam asked for both of us.

"Yeah."

I got excited and scared all at once.

"They're not gonna make a decision until Monday."

"That sucks!" I said loudly. There was a moment of

silence, followed by bursts of laughter from Pete and Sam. Their laughter got me laughing, too. I knew they were laughing at how funny I sounded swearing. It was a clear case of laughter telepathy—where you all get the joke without anyone having to say it.

"Ze young man must learn ze patience, yah," Sam said with a German accent.

"Yah," I repeated.

Then the three of us: "Yah, yah."

We all went down to the soundstage for the run-through. As was the case the previous week, the writers, director, and various tech people moved in a group to whatever part of the set was being used for a particular scene. Neal Peachy was among the writers scribbling notes in their scripts. This was his day to come in and help as much as possible with the punch-up. From the way things were going, it looked like the script could use his help. The story of Grace finding her real mom on the Internet was fairly serious, so most of the laughs were going to have to come from Tom Parker supplying Marisol with dating tips, giving her date the once-over, and him helping the little kids set up their tent in the backyard. It could be a late night in the writer's room.

The run-through had come late that day, so when we returned to the production bungalow, dinner was waiting for us outside the room. The writers had carted their catered meals into the room, wanting to get right to work on the punch-up. Sam had gone home with Kari, so I took my chicken parmigiana and several chocolate chip cookies into Pete's office and turned on the TV. It was Thursday night, just past eight, so of course a rerun of *Kids* was on. It was the one where Tom is giving Devin driving lessons and ends up knocking over the fire hydrant in front of their house. The little kids were all running through the shower of water when Pete's phone rang. It was my mom.

"I'm sorry, honey. Those ruins are not easy to get to, let me tell you. We were trapped in the jungle until seven. I just got your message. You sounded like something was wrong. Is it about the part?"

"No. They're not going to decide till Monday. Mom, Dad thinks I'm at the Y."

"What? I don't understand."

"I never asked him if I could hang out at the studio instead of going to day camp. I was afraid he'd say I couldn't go, and then I wouldn't have had a chance of getting on the show."

"Oh, sweetie," she sighed. It was a "my son's fallen in a pit of mischief" sigh. "What am I going to do with you?" Her tone then changed. She was mad, but not at me. "If your father weren't so stubborn, always thinking he was the only one who had an opinion that mattered, you wouldn't feel like you had to lie to him. Not that that excuses what you've done. I'll call him in the morning and then have him to talk to you."

"He'll never let me be on the show now."

"You shouldn't have lied, especially to me . . ."

"I didn't lie. It was really more of an omission."

"Let's not get fancy here, you know you avoided telling me the truth."

"Yeah, I'm sorry."

"I'm going to see if I can get a flight to L.A. tomorrow. You need me there. Besides, I think Raphael wants to see Hollywood. He likes you a lot, you know."

My mom's pretty cool as far as moms go. Of course, then there's Raphael, and I have to wonder about her whole decision-making ability.

"I'll call Pete and let him know when we'll be in. Don't worry, honey, everything will be all right. I love you."

"I love you, too, Mom."

"Oh, by the way, there was a message on my home machine from some agent, a Walter something, do you know anything about that?"

"Just someone Sam introduced me to."

"He wanted to talk about representing you. He seemed to think that your getting this role on the show was—how did he put it?—in the bag."

I didn't have to wait long on Friday to hear from my dad. As soon as we walked into the production office, Bonnie gave me the message that he had called and to call him back immediately. He obviously now knew that I wasn't at the Y.

I went into Pete's office and punched in my dad's number. A woman answered the phone: "Blaine & Stewart, how may I direct your call?"

"Hi, Janine, it's Tyler. Is my dad there?"

"Hi, Tyler. Hold on, he's expecting your call." There was a pause for a few moments, during which I was sure my dad was telling Janine to hold all his other calls. Then his voice came on the line. It was his stern "you're in trouble, son" voice.

"Tyler."

"Hi, Dad."

"Do you have something you want to tell me?" Typical of my dad: He knew what I had done but wanted to make me say it.

"Yeah. I'm sorry for not telling you that I wasn't going to the Y."

"You lied to me, son."

"I never really—"

"Tyler, if you're going to learn from this, then you're going to have to be truthful starting right now. You purposely deceived me." I should have known that my "technically it was an omission" dodge would just make him angrier at me.

"Yeah, I did," I admitted.

"Good."

"I did really well at my audition."

"So your mother tells me, but that's not what we're talking about now."

Silence. Then my dad saying, "Hello?" *(Earth to Tyler, Earth to Tyler.)*

"Yeah."

"I want you to promise me that you'll never do anything like this again, and I want you to mean it."

"I promise."

"This whole thing has spun completely out of control. I've gotten calls from three agents."

"If I get this part, and I might 'cause everyone says I did really well—"

"We'll see. I'm flying out there on Monday."

"Mom's coming today."

"I know, but I need to be there, too, especially if any legal issues need to be handled."

"You mean, it's okay with you that I—"

"No, it's not okay, but I want to wait until I'm out there before making a final judgment."

I suddenly felt like I was in some courtroom drama, standing before my father, the judge. He'd be dressed in a black robe and, if the show was British, a frilly white wig. *But I'm your son,* I'd plead. *The law's the law,* he'd say. *I sentence you to a life of boredom. Court adjourned.*

"Dad, it's not as bad out here as you think."

"You've been in that town for, what, a week, and you're already lying to me."

"It's not Hollywood's fault—"

"We'll talk about it on Monday. Tyler, you're not a child anymore. It's important that you learn to take responsibility for your actions. Are you with me here?"

"Yes, Dad."

"I'll see you on Monday."

I hung up the phone. I was now feeling totally lousy. I had thought that by not telling my dad what was really going on, I'd be increasing my chances of getting on the show, but now I realized that by, all right, lying to him, I was only confirming his worst impressions of Hollywood.

Pete walked in. "I just talked to your mom," he said. "They're getting in at three o'clock." I must have been looking pretty pouty, 'cause he then said, "You did the right thing. Everything's going to be okay. Don't be so hard on your dad. He's just doing what he thinks is best for you."

"That's what I'm afraid of," I said.

Sam was at her tennis lesson, so I went over to the soundstage and watched rehearsal. I thought about what Pete had just said. What did he mean, don't be too hard on your dad? I'd never thought I could be too hard on my dad. I only thought he was always too hard on me. It didn't make sense.

So there I sat in the bleachers along with the stand-ins and extras with their paperback novels to occupy them while they waited to be used. I was beginning to realize that this waiting thing was a big part of what acting was all about. First you waited to get an agent. Then you waited for an audition. If you got one of those, you waited to find out if you'd gotten a callback. Then, if you got called back, you waited to see if you'd gotten the part. You'd think that would end all the waiting, but you'd be wrong. Once you did get cast, even in a big part, you stood around the set waiting for the camera people and other technicians to get things just right or for the director to figure out where he wanted you or the cameras to go, so that you could finally rehearse your scene. Then, for the next scene, the whole waiting process would be repeated. That was if you were in the next scene, 'cause if you weren't, then all you could do was wait until there was a scene that you were in.

I'd have to wait the entire weekend now to find out if I'd made it onto the show. Was my whole life about to change? I'd have to wait and see. And would my parents allow my life to change, even if that was exactly what Baxter Rhodes, Jerry Stone, and all the studio and network suits wanted? I'd have to wait and see.

Sam showed up in the afternoon, and I told her everything about my conversations with my mom and dad. "Well, he didn't say you couldn't do it," she mused while sipping an ice tea. We were sitting at a table in front of the Back Lot Café. Every ten minutes or so a Universal tour bus would go by, not to mention a steady stream of golf carts. "And he's a lawyer, so you don't have to have an agent with you to make a deal. More money for your trust fund."

"How does that work?"

"You trust that your parents don't blow all your money before you turn twenty-one."

My mom and Raphael were due in at LAX at three. Since Friday at four was when *Kids* had its network run-through, Pete couldn't pick them up, so they were going to have to take a cab to the studio.

Once again everyone moved in a pack from scene to scene, but this time with the addition of the network suits. One of the suits was from Standards and Practices. He was the censor. Since our show was an eight o'clock family show, it had to be really clean. You couldn't really talk like people talked in real life; you had to be on cable to do that.

No one was saying anything to me about the part. I wasn't even getting a smug "It's in the bag" from Eddie McNamara or a sweet "I hope you get it" from Faith Remo. Had everyone caught Kari's superstitious bug? Jerry Stone, as usual, ignored me. Did they know something I didn't? Sam was telling me not to read too much into what people were or were not saying, when I spotted Bonnie leading my mom and Raphael across the soundstage floor to where we were standing. They looked like they'd just stepped out of the jungle—after a trip to Banana Republic. I have to tell you, it was great to see my mom. Raphael I could have done without. The first thing I noticed was how tanned they were, my mom in particular. Her newly darkened skin stood out in contrast to her blond hair, as opposed to Raphael, whose olive skin matched his long black hair perfectly. "I missed you so much," she said as she wrapped me up in a big hug. Then she was hugging Pete, who had joined our group, while Raphael was mussing up my hair going, "Hey, it's the next Macaulay Culkin." Leave it to Raphael to pick some has-been from the last century to compare me to.

I introduced Sam, and my mom hugged her like she was a member of the family. "I've heard a lot about you," she said.

"Your mother is the actress, yes?" Raphael interjected.

"So I've read in *TV Guide*," Sam said dryly.

Raphael looked confused. My mom helped him out. "It's a joke, Raphael."

"Yep, all we do around here is make jokes and have fun all day long, right, guys?" Pete quipped.

"Okay, now I know you're yanking on my leg."

"Pulling, honey," my mom corrected him.

"Right." He then waved a finger at Pete and said, "I know you work hard to make everyone laugh."

"Here she is now," Sam said, pointing to Kari, who was striding toward our little group.

More introductions and "I've heard so much about yous" followed. The string of pleasantries was interrupted, however, when Kari said, "That was quite a scare we all got the other night when Tyler had that awful asthma attack. You must worry about him all the time."

There was an awkward silence. My mom looked at me and then at Pete. "Well, maybe it was a little more serious than we let on," he said. "We didn't want you to worry, being so far away and all."

"Um-hm" was all my mom said.

We then gave my mom and Raphael a little tour of the set and production offices, but I knew that when we got back to Pete's apartment that "um-hm" would turn into a full-blown lecture about our well-intentioned if not completely honest downplay.

21

Pete and I had planned to do some sort of outing with Kari and Sam on Saturday. Now that my mom and Raphael were in town we'd all be going together.

My mom made breakfast—when the bacon and eggs had entered Pete's beverage-only refrigerator, I have no idea—and the four us tried to figure out where to go for the day. Pete thought Kari might still want to go to the TV museum. Raphael wanted to go to Mann's Chinese Theatre and walk the Hollywood Walk of Fame, but Pete didn't think that would be such a good idea since Kari would undoubtedly be mobbed by fans. My mom didn't care what we did. I think her brain was working on the problem of what to do if I got cast in the show. My brain was already overworked from thinking about it, so it was good to have someone else on the case.

Raphael was taking a shower and Pete and I were washing the dishes when my mom asked Pete, "So what's going on with you and Kari?" My mom was never one for finesse.

"Oh, um, nothing."

"A big star like that isn't going to play tour guide for the likes of us unless there's something going on, and I do think there's something going on."

"There's nothing going on. Really. We're just hanging out because of Tyler and Sam."

140

"I think she likes you," my mom continued. "I'm an expert at picking up vibes between people, and there's definitely a vibe between the two of you."

If there *was* a vibe between Pete and Kari, he'd probably be the last one in the country to figure it out. Pete never thought anyone was interested in him, let alone the likes of Kari Franklin.

It was decided that we'd meet Sam and Kari in Griffith Park near the entrance on Fern Dell and then hike up to the observatory.

Sam and I led the way on the hike. I told her what my mom had said about her mom and Pete. "Could be," she said. "Though it's hard to believe she's developed good taste in men after all the creeps she's dated."

"Like Raphael?"

"Raphael's not a creep. I think he's hot," Sam said, turning around to look at Raphael.

"Do you lu-u-uv him?" I said, getting revenge for all Sam's Faith Remo teasing.

"No, but he *is* hot."

Once we'd gotten up to the observatory, we checked out what our weight would be on Mars and the moon and watched this pendulum swing back and forth in a huge pit, slowly knocking down pins. Pete said it had something to do with Earth's magnetic field, but I just thought it looked cool.

The whole time we were there, only one person came up to Kari to tell her how great she was, though every once in a while I'd see someone whisper to whoever they were with after she had walked by them.

When we were back outside and walking down the observatory steps, Raphael suddenly realized that we were in the very spot where they'd shot *Rebel Without a Cause*. He then went into a James Dean impression that, filtered through his Italian accent, had us all laughing. I'd never seen him be funny before, at least not on purpose. Sam was impressed. "Totally hot," she said.

We hiked down to our cars and then headed over to the Museum of Television and Radio in Beverly Hills. I rode with Kari and Sam.

"Tyler's mom thinks there's a vibe between you and Pete," Sam blurted out. She said the word "vibe" like it was something really spooky.

"If there is, that's between me and Pete and none of your business, young lady."

Sam turned around to me and said, "I believe that's a confirmation. You're gonna need a tux for the wedding."

"Sam!"

"Mom!"

At the museum we split up into singles or pairs and ordered different videos to watch on our own private monitors. I picked some early *Kids* episodes. In them Kari and Jerry Stone were way younger. I think Jerry still had his original hair, 'cause you could see it thinning in places. Eddie McNamara was about eight years old, and adorable as the then-youngest member of the Parker household. The other five original kids had now all left the house. You might see them on an occasional reunion episode, but outside of that their acting careers were pretty much over. I wondered if being on *Kids* would forever be the highlight of their lives. I wondered if I were to get on the show if it would be the highlight of mine. It seemed pretty sad to think that a person's life could peak at seventeen.

Kari and Pete were listening to some old radio broadcasts of her dad. Everyone else had finished up with what they were watching, so we all listened in as her father, no older than Sam or me, played the squeaky-voiced son in *Lucky and Flo*, a hit radio program from the forties.

Kari treated us all to dinner at Jerry's Famous Deli, where we all pigged out on burgers and corned beef sandwiches—except for Sam, who had a tuna salad. She did, however, have her share of french fries.

"Is your father still alive?" my mom asked Kari.

"Oh, yeah, he and my mom still live in the house I grew up in, in Brentwood. He was a writer too." She threw a glance over to Pete. "Wrote for some of the best shows ever in the sixties and seventies. He still teaches a class out of the house."

"What does he think of what's on TV today?" my mom asked.

"He thinks most of it is crap, but he's always thought that most of it is crap."

"And what does he think of your show?" Raphael asked.

"Sometimes he thinks it's good and other times . . ."

"Crap. It's a bunch of crap," Sam grumbled in an old man's voice, and everyone laughed.

. . .

143

It had been a totally fun day. I was even starting to like Raphael a little bit after seeing him through Sam's eyes. My good mood was quickly deflated, however, when we got home and listened to the message my dad had left on Pete's voice mail: "Pete, it's Frank. Would you let Laura and Tyler know that I'll be getting in on Monday afternoon? I should be at the studio by around four, so we'll talk about this business with your show at that time. And I'll need you to leave my name at the gate. Don't forget. Thanks."

"He's scheduling an appointment with us," my mom said in exasperation. "Can you believe that?"

"He still thinks your family's a corporation and he's the chairman," Pete half-joked.

"He's lucky he still even has a say in what Tyler does or doesn't do." My mom was starting to boil. Raphael made the mistake of trying to calm her down.

"I'm sure things are not so bad. I think he must listen to reason."

"Raphael, please. You have no idea what Frank is like. Just stay out of this, all right?"

She then turned to me. "Are you okay, honey?"

"Yeah, I'm fine." I then went into the bathroom and launched a couple of sprays from my inhaler into my lungs.

By the next morning, my mom had cooled down, and things between her and Raphael seemed to be back to normal.

Pete needed to spend the day writing, so my mom, Raphael, and I took the Corolla and drove to the beach in Santa Monica.

The heat of summer was still with us, even by the ocean. We had barely laid out our beach towels and set down the ice chest, which had ham-and-cheese sand-wiches and sodas, and beer for Raphael, when my mom turned to me and said, "Let's go for a walk." She'd obvi-ously planned this little "alone time," for Raphael just said, "Have a nice time," then turned onto his stomach and started soaking up sun.

"So on a scale of one to ten, how are you liking Raphael these days?" my mom asked as we walked along the ocean, our legs getting sprayed by the incom-ing waves.

"Well, he's worked his way up from a two to almost a five."

"I know he's a little young for me, but he's very sweet and he treats me nice."

"Sam thinks he's hot."

"Does she, now? I'm glad you two have become such good friends."

"Yeah, me too."

I knew that talking about Sam and Raphael was just a warm-up for a talk about my dad and what might happen tomorrow when the network finally made its decision about who was to be cast as the new kid in the house.

"I know how much you want to be in the show and I am so proud of you for getting this far, but have you thought about what you might have to give up if you do get the part?"

"A little bit," I said. "I know we'd have to move out here."

"That's true. I'd have to find a new job, a new house for us. You wouldn't be able to go to a regular school; you'd have to be taught at the studio. You'd have a full-time job in addition to your schoolwork. It's not an easy life. I'm sure you can tell that just from the time you've been staying here with Pete." She was right about that. These kids did put in some pretty full days, and I was seeing them in summer; just wait till school started.

"You wouldn't see Frog or any of your other friends back home," she continued, "and though I know it sounds great to have people recognize you, that can also be a burden." On my way out to L.A. all I could think about was how great it would be to be famous. But ever since Sam had mentioned it as a real possibility, while we were waiting for the T2 show to begin, I'd been gnawed at by the thought that no one would know me for me anymore; they'd know me for this character I played on TV. And just like I'd found out with every one of the kids and adults in the show, these were all real people whose personalities sometimes had little to do with the image that was projected into people's living rooms across America. I couldn't quite put this into words, however, while my mom and I walked down the beach that day. All I could say was "Kari had to put a restraining order on some guy who was stalking her."

Then we talked about my dad.

"Your father is a difficult person... very frustrating to deal with, but he does love you. A lot of other parents would see this as an opportunity to make a lot of money, but he wants what's best for you in the long term."

"How can he know that being on the show won't be good for me?"

"He doesn't and neither do I. And neither do you right now, but we have to use our experience and judgment to make the best decision we can."

I knew that from my dad's point of view that would mean not letting me be in the show.

We walked in silence for a while.

"He didn't even care that they liked me and called me back."

"He cares. He just doesn't know how to show it. That's why I couldn't live with him anymore. He had a way of making me feel like I was always failing, and to see him do that to you..." She broke off, holding back tears. "Come on, let's go back," she said, still a little shaky.

She didn't mention my dad or the show for the rest of the day.

I couldn't sleep that night. My brain was swirling with questions. Would I get the part? Would my dad refuse to let me do it? Would my mom insist that I did? Would getting on the show be as great as I'd thought it would be? When I finally did fall asleep, I had a very strange dream: I was with Frog, swimming in his pool. My cell phone started ringing. I said hello and there was no one there. Then I was inside the house. Suddenly I was no longer at Frog's but in our house outside Chicago, only it looked all different. It was bigger. I walked into the living room. The TV was on. Sitting on the couch, drinking a cherry cola, was Jerry Stone. I thought he was going to ignore me, as usual, but then he turned to me and said, "Poof, you're gone."

I opened my eyes and sat up. Pete was on the futon, lightly snoring. The clock next to the couch I was on said three-thirty.

I plopped back down, wondering what Dr. Von Head-shrinker would say: *Ze boy's gone funny in ze head, yah.*

"Yah, yah."

"**It's** just anxiety," Sam said when I told her about my dream. I'd found her Monday morning by the craft service table, filling up a plate with fruit. "Don't worry about it. You look wasted."

"I slept for, like, five minutes," I said, "and that's when I had that stupid dream. You want to come with me, my mom, and Raphael up to CityWalk?"

"Sure."

So Bonnie and one of the other P.A.s put the four of us in their golf carts and drove us up the hill to the back entrance of Universal's CityWalk. As we were going from shop to shop and munching on whatever snacks were in our path, Baxter Rhodes was meeting with the network suits to decide who would be cast as the next kid in the house.

Before we'd left for the studio that morning, my mom had said to me, "Don't worry about your father. I'll handle him."

It looked like she was going to get her chance, for when we came back to the production bungalow, there, sitting in Pete's office talking on the phone and looking like he was about to walk into a big corporate meeting in his dark suit and tie, was my dad.

"Just reschedule that for next week. What day are we in court with Jacobson?"

He did a kind of "be with you in a minute" wave with his hand that immediately pushed one of my mom's many buttons. "Frank, get off the phone."

"Janine, I've got to go. I'll call you in a few hours." He hung up the phone. "You weren't here, so I thought I'd take care of some business."

"Can't waste a moment, can we?" My dad just ignored my mom's dig.

"Hey, Tyler, how are you?"

"I'm okay."

Just then Pete walked into the room. I thought he might have some news about the part, but all he said was "Oh, good, you're back." He might as well have said *Oh boy, here we go.*

Sam, never one to miss an exit cue, said, "Come on, Raphael, let's go down and watch them set the cameras." I don't think Sam was too upset at having to chaperone Raphael.

"Pete, maybe you should go too," my dad said.

"No, he stays," my mom said. "He's part of this family and understands better than any of us what it will mean if they want Tyler to be in the show." It was clear that my mom was in battle mode and why she'd been so quiet since our walk on the beach: She'd been conserving her energy for this moment, for this confrontation with my dad.

"All right," my dad said, but he remained sitting in the "power position" behind Pete's desk.

Pete closed the door and pulled up a chair. My mom and I were on the sofa.

My dad focused on me. "Tyler, I know this means a lot to you, but just because we want something doesn't mean it's the right thing for us. I just don't think this is a good environment for you to grow up in. It's already had a negative impact on you—thinking it was all right to lie to both me and your mother, even Pete here, all because you wanted to be on TV."

"He lied because he was afraid of you," My mom responded. "Afraid you'd not let him do something that he's good at because of your holier-than-thou attitude."

"Lying is lying."

"You haven't said a word to him about what's he's accomplished. About how much talent he has. We wouldn't even be having this conversation if he weren't good."

"That's not the point."

"That is the point. That is exactly the point. You don't support him in a way that's healthy."

"You think it's healthy to let him have a couple of years of glory, and then what? I'll tell you." My dad's eyes narrowed as he leaned forward. "He'll only have the vices he's learned to fall back on."

"Not everyone out here is bad," I said, suddenly finding my voice. "Sure there's some creeps, but there's some pretty nice people too. To me it doesn't seem that different from anywhere else I've been."

There was a brief silence, broken by my dad saying, in a very respectful voice, "Tyler, would you mind if your mother and I talk alone for a few minutes?" My mom gave me an "it's okay" nod and Pete rose and said, "Come on, pal, I'll go with you."

I was shaking when we got outside. "You okay?" Pete asked as we sat on one of the sofas just outside the writers' room. "Yeah," I said. But I wasn't. It seemed that my mom and dad had been fighting over what was best for me for as long as I could remember. That hadn't changed with their divorce.

It was obvious to Pete, though, that I wasn't okay. "Hey, I know things seem horrible right now—" he began to say, but was interrupted by Baxter Rhodes's angry voice coming up the stairwell. Close behind him were several other of the show's high-end writers. "The sheer stupidity of these people, I cannot believe!" Baxter was clearly in the midst of a rant. "Where do they come up with these things? It's not that the network hires idiots that bothers me. I understand, idiots need jobs, too. It's that they listen to them." He and his small group were about to enter the writers' room when he stopped and focused on Pete and me. "Come on in, Pete. Tyler, you should come, too. You can learn something about the stupidity that goes on around here."

We followed them into the writers' room, where the rest of the writing staff waited in anticipation of whatever bad news Baxter was about to deliver. He walked to the front and heaved a great sigh. "We have to come up with another kid," he said.

This statement was followed by a chorus of "what"s and curses from the other writers.

My mind was racing. What did he mean, another kid? Did they need to hold more auditions for the part of Ben? Could my dad have already said something that had caused me to lose the part? It soon became clear, however, that it wasn't another actor they needed to find but another character.

"They were afraid that this was going to cause them more trouble than it was worth," Baxter said as he waved about a piece of paper. "Some VP in publicity sent this memo to the head of comedy. Listen to this." He began reading: "The County Department of Social Services, who have always supported the show in the past, would not support our portrayal of them as incapable of meeting the needs of one of the children in their system. In addition, the fact that this child has gone from one home to another draws a picture of adoptive and foster parents who are unqualified and unwilling to deal with the problems of the children in their care."

"But the kid's going to turn it around at the Parkers'," Sherry protested.

"But according to this imbecile, we imply that all the other families are crappy ones," Baxter said.

"That's insane," someone else yelled out.

"Wait a second," Pete said. "How does the Department of Social Services even know what we're planning?"

"They don't," Baxter said, a tinge of anger coming back into his voice.

Suddenly Baxter was looking right at me. "See, Tyler," he said, "this is how it works: Some middle-management moron thinks that perhaps, maybe, someone from the county might be offended by something we want to do on the show. They then start sending out e-mails to everyone in programming about the damage this might do to the network and the show. They might even get legal involved. Now we're talking lawsuits. Someone on top then says, 'It's not worth it. Write another part.' And that's it. Has anyone from the county actually complained? No. Would they have complained if the episode had aired? I really don't think so."

"Poor kid, can't even get adopted by a TV family," Ellen joked.

Everyone just sat there for a few moments. I was trying to absorb what Baxter had just said. The only thing that seemed clear was that the part of Ben was now history. My fate hadn't been decided by my dad or mom or Jerry Stone or even myself. Some person who I'd never met, who didn't even seem to have a name, who didn't even know I existed, had ruined my chances of getting on the show. I was numb.

"All right," Baxter finally said, looking at the chalkboard, "where are we with this story?"

"Come on, let's tell your folks what's going on," Pete whispered to me. We were almost out the door when Baxter said, "Oh, Tyler, this may be of small consolation, but I thought you were the best. Maybe we can use you for something else sometime."

"Thanks," I said, and walked out of the room with Pete.

My parents were still arguing when Pete and I reentered his office. Pete told them what had just happened. My mom comforted me with a big hug and a "I'm so sorry, honey. I know how much it meant to you." I was numb. My dad put his hand on my shoulder and said, "I'm sorry, too, Tyler, but I think in the long run you'll see that this may have turned out for the best." I could see that my mom was ready give my dad a hard time about his "turned out for the best" comment but decided to let it go. Instead she said, "Let's go home."

Pete handed her the car keys, saying that he'd get a ride home from one of the other writers. "Where's Raphael?" she asked.

"With Sam," I said. "I'll go find them."

"Tyler, how about we spend the day together tomorrow?" my dad asked.

"Okay," I said, "but can we can get back early? Tomorrow's tape night."

"Sure, son."

I was walking from the production office to the soundstage when I saw Sam and Raphael headed my way. They had heard the news about the part being scratched. "That totally bites," Sam said.

"I feel bad for you, Tyler, but look how close you got," Raphael said. "If you got close this time, then next time for sure." At that moment I didn't expect there would be a next time. I'd really felt that this was my big chance, and now it was gone. The day after next was when I was supposed to go back to Chicago. I had thought I'd be coming right back to be on the show, but now who knew when I'd see Sam or Kari again? "We have to go home," I said to Raphael. I wanted to say more to Sam, but with Raphael there all I could do was look at her and go, "Thanks for your help."

"I'll see you tomorrow, right?"

"I'll be at the taping," I said.

"Hey, it could be worse," Sam called out as we were walking away.

I turned back to her. "Yeah, how?"

Sam shrugged. "I don't know. I was just trying to make you feel better."

My mom cooked spaghetti and meatballs, my favorite, for dinner. As Raphael cleaned up afterward, she said all the right things to me: about how proud she was of me, and that if this was something I really wanted to do, she'd make sure I got into some classes once we were back home, and that my dad's inability to give me the support and encouragement I needed was his problem and not mine. I still felt pretty lousy, however.

I sent off an e-mail to Frog telling him how I'd come to lose the part of a lifetime—albeit a short lifetime. I figured that by the time I saw him again, he'd have come up with at least a half dozen examples of TV network blundering in an effort to cheer me up. Frog was a good friend.

My mom and Raphael had gone to sleep but I was still awake, thinking about how close I'd come, when I heard the unmistakable purr of a Jaguar from the street below. I got up and went over to the window and saw Pete getting out of Kari's car. Maybe there really was something going on between him and Kari. A minute later he walked in.

"Can't sleep, huh?" he said upon seeing me.

"No."

"You hungry?"

"Yeah."

"I'm starving, myself." I followed Pete into the kitchen. "Wow, this concept of keeping food actually in the house, quite a leap forward for mankind, don't you think?" He fixed us each a ham-and-cheese sandwich slathered with mustard and mayonnaise, and we sat down at the dining room table.

"I know it's tough right now, all this craziness with your mom and dad," Pete said somberly. "And now losing this part, on what amounts to a technicality, but one day, I promise, you're gonna look back on this and laugh, and I'm not just saying this to make you feel better. In fact, this could all be great comedy material."

"Yeah, right."

"I'm serious. It's classic banana peel."

"What?"

"Classic banana peel. Look, it's not so funny when you're the guy slipping on the banana peel, but when it's somebody else, you laugh, right?"

"Yeah."

"Well, it's the same with this; after a while you'll start to see it from a different perspective, and a lot of it's going to seem pretty funny—you'll even laugh at yourself."

I tried to wrap my brain around what Pete was saying but quickly came back to the disappointment I was still immersed in. "Everyone kept saying it was in the bag," I said. "I hate 'in the bag.' 'In the bag' sucks."

"Yeah, it does," Pete said. "It really does."

Well, I was finally going to The The Tar Tar Pits. My dad had picked me up in his rented BMW at around ten on Tuesday morning. My mom, Raphael, and I would be flying back to Chicago the following day. My mom kept saying that it was a good idea for me to spend the day with my dad. "Maybe you can resolve some things . . . I don't know, but it's best if you don't go home angry at him." I really didn't want to spend the day with my dad. I would have preferred to hang out with Sam at the studio; after all, it was the last day I'd be seeing her.

As we drove through the Cahuenga Pass and onto Highland Avenue, my dad said nothing about what had occurred the day before. Instead he talked about what we would do when I visited him in New York over Labor Day. "The Cubs will be in town. I thought we could take in a game. I also though about going up to Lake Placid for a couple of days, maybe rent a boat, do some fishing. Remember when we went fishing that time? What do you think?" My dad was clearly in his hot-fudge-sundae mode.

"Sure. That sounds great," I said.

We arrived at the La Brea Tar Pits. It was in a park next to the L.A. County Museum of Art. We looked at the replicated woolly mammoths screaming, unable to extricate themselves from the tar that they had mistaken for a fresh drink of water. They must have been pretty clueless to mistake this thick black sludge for water. No wonder they were extinct. We went inside the Page Museum and checked out the real fossils of the mammoths, saber-toothed tigers, and various birds, all of whom had made the same blunder with tar.

As we walked back through the park to the car, I was hoping that my dad would say something about being proud of me for being talented and almost making it onto a network show, having out-auditioned all those other kids. But he didn't. He continued to talk about things we could do in New York and some new software he was going to get me for the coming school year.

When I tried to look at it from his point of view, it made total sense: How could he be impressed by what I had done when he had so little respect for the people who had been impressed by me? But instead of this realization making me feel worse about everything, I found it somehow liberating. *He just doesn't get it, that's all,* I thought. For the first time all of my mom's "You may never please your father"s and all of her "It's not your fault"s made sense. We were just different, and his displeasure with me had more to do with what *he* might be missing than with what *I* might have done wrong.

We walked on past various parkgoers sitting on benches and a guy playing something classical on a clarinet, whose open case contained a few small bills and some change. The music sounded sweet, so I pulled a couple of quarters out of my pocket and tossed them in his case.

We got back to the studio just in time for the taping. Bonnie escorted my dad to a seat in the bleachers next to my mom and Raphael. I waved to Pete, who was huddled in a group with Baxter Rhodes and the other writers. I was back by the craft service table looking for Sam when I walked right into—you guessed it—Jerry Stone. I was expecting a "Get out of my way, kid" at the very best, but instead Jerry said, "Come over here a second." He pulled me away from everyone else and said, "You were the best one we saw for the part. I'm sorry it didn't work out." He gave me a pat on the shoulder like I was one of his TV kids and walked off. I was shocked. Jerry Stone thought I was good—and had told me so. He wasn't the only one. I hadn't realized how many people had been rooting for me to get on the show until it slipped out of my grasp. The P.A.s, some tech people I'd met, Faith Remo, and Eddie McNamara all offered me their condolences. I even think Eddie was sincere about it.

Sam was with Kari in her dressing room. Kari, who hadn't said a word to me about my audition because of her fear of jinxes, now gave me a big hug. "I was so nervous for you," she said. "I'm sorry things didn't work out the way you wanted, but maybe this just wasn't meant to be. When something like this happens, I always say: One door closes and another one opens."

"Can we spare him the New Age philosophy, Mom?" Sam said.

"It's not New Age philosophy. It's good sound advice.

You're too young to be this jaded. Where did I go wrong?" she said with mock concern.

"I think it started with all those Shirley MacLaine books."

Someone came by to tell Kari that she needed to get in place for the preshow introductions. "Well, I'm sure we'll see you again soon," Kari said warmly to me.

I just nodded and said, "Break a leg."

"Thank you," Kari said, and left the room.

Sam pulled a grocery bag out from under Kari's makeup counter. "Hey, I got you a going-away present. Here," she said. Inside was a black leather jacket with *Kids in the House* stitched in blue letters on the back. "Wow! This is so cool!" I said, holding it up.

"Put it on," Sam said. I got into the jacket. "You look awesome," she said.

I checked myself out in the mirror. I *did* look pretty cool, I have to admit.

From the stage I could hear the amplified voice of tonight's stand-up saying, "And now, let's meet the cast of *Kids in the House*." The audience cheered and applauded.

"Let's go," Sam said. She started to head for the door, but I remained where I was. Sam stopped. "What?" she asked.

"Thanks," I said.

"No problem. Come on." As Sam closed the dressing-room door behind us, she said, "Hey, guess what?"

"What?"

"Somewhere a door just opened." Laughing, we made our way to the stage.

The warm-up comedian had worked the crowd up, and they were ready to "feed the actors energy," as he put it. They pelted the actors with their cheers as each was introduced. After Jerry and Kari had been announced to huge applause, the guy with the slate board announced the first scene, the director said, "Action!" and we were on our way.

Sam and I were on the floor, watching most of the scenes on one of the monitors or carefully viewing the action through the cracks in between all the cameras and people who were actually working.

This episode was the beginning of the end for Gretchen Harris and her character, Grace. Even though the trades had been reporting that Gretchen would be leaving *Kids,* no one who wasn't connected with the show knew exactly how that was going to come about. It was all being saved for the November sweeps. So when Grace told Colby Parker that she had been in contact over the Internet with her birth mom, a low ripple of *aahs* went through the audience. The mood of that story was contrasted by Tom Parker getting all flustered over Marisol's first date: *If he tries to kiss you, turn your head quickly away. Like this.* Tom then tries to demonstrate but ends up getting a muscle spasm in his neck. Jerry, of course, pulled this off brilliantly and sent the audience into howls of laughter. His antics of dealing with his neck continued throughout the show. Watching him help the little kids pitch a tent in the backyard was hysterically funny. I looked up to the bleachers; even my dad was laughing.

As the actors went from scene to scene, I couldn't help but think how close I'd come to being up there myself. But I also thought about what Kari had said. Maybe it just wasn't meant to be, at least not right now. Who knew, maybe another opportunity would come up when things were more right. After all, Baxter had said that they might be able to use me for something else.

The taping quickly went by until there was only one scene left to do. Tom, unable to resist making sure that Marisol's date didn't try anything "funny," had ended up in the tent with the younger kids, where he had a clear view of the front porch. When they went out of his sight line, he and his stiff neck slowly crept into the bushes by the porch. Still unable to see what was going on, he scaled a tree whose branches hovered over the porch. He peered down to see Marisol about to get a big kiss on the lips. Marisol's eyes flashed and she let out a scream. She had spotted Tom in the tree, and now he came tumbling out of it, landing on the porch between Marisol and her date. Jerry, the master of the pratfall, had once again sent the audience into fits of laughter. By now all the other members of the Parker household were on the porch, wanting to see what was going on. Tom very slowly and very painfully, going through complex contortions because of his now even more spasmed neck, got to his feet, looked at everyone staring at him, opened his mouth to speak and then, thinking better of it, turned and stiffly walked into the house. There was mild laughter throughout the audience. The director said, "Cut!" The audience applauded. Baxter, Pete, Neal Peachy, and the other writers were standing in front of me and Sam. "I knew that wasn't going to work," Baxter said, shaking his head. "He's got to say something." The writers started pitching lines to Baxter:

"Nice to meet you, I'm Tom Parker. Welcome to my porch," said Neal.

"So kids, how was the movie?" It was Pete this time.

"My daughter for an aspirin?" Sherry threw in.

"Excuse me, I think I left my dignity in the house," said Neal again.

"This tree will definitely not support a tree house," a voice said. It was my voice. The words had just shot out of my mouth before I knew what I doing, like when I'd made that comment about Jerry's hair transplant. Only this time the surprised looks on everyone's faces was followed by Baxter saying, "That's good. Let's try that." He walked over to Jerry and told him the line. Jerry nodded and then climbed back onto the tree branch, which had been reset while the writers had been pitching. Faith Remo and the actor playing her date returned to the porch while everyone else went to where they would be entering from. The guy with the slate board announced the scene, and the director said, "Action!" Once again Marisol screamed and Tom Parker came tumbling out of the tree. Once again the other Parker family members rushed to the porch, and once again Jerry, as Tom, went through a complex series of contortions in order to get to his feet, Only this time, through obvious pain he looked up at the tree and said, "This tree will definitely not support a tree house." The audience howled with laughter and then, as before, Tom turned and stiffly walked through the front door of the house. The director said "Cut" and the audience burst into booming applause.

The taping was over, except for some pickup shots that would be done after the audience had been cleared from the building. The warm-up guy brought the cast out one at a time for curtain calls. They all rose to their feet when Jerry came running to the front and took a bow, first alone, and then with the entire cast.

Sam was ecstatic. "That was so-o-o cool! You came up with the blow to the show!"

There was a rush of people around me The writers were all giving me high fives and telling me I rocked. Baxter Rhodes said, "I owe you one, Tyler" Jerry Stone came up to me and shook my hand. "Nice work, kid," he said. "That's my kind of line." He walked off, saying, "Is it me, or are the writers in this town getting younger?"

Pete must have told my parents and Raphael that the line they'd heard Jerry Stone deliver had first sprung out of my brain. "Such a talented kid," Raphael was saying. "Brilliant! Brilliant!" My mom gave me a big hug and was crying. "I am so proud of you," she said through her tears.

"Come on, Mom," I said.

My dad had joined us. He had a big grin on his face. "How did you come up with that line?" he asked.

"I don't know. It just sounded funny in my head, and I guess it had to come out."

Pete and his Corolla took us to the airport the next morning. My dad had taken the red-eye back to New York. I'd be seeing him again in a couple of weeks, and for the first time in a while I was actually looking forward to it. He'd still been talking about my ability to come up with that line for Jerry Stone as he'd gotten into his rented BMW and driven away. As for Sam, we'd said good-bye the night before as well. In the two weeks or so that I'd been in Hollywood, Sam had gone from someone who I hadn't even known existed to being one of my best friends; maybe, with the exception of Frog, my best. Neither one of us had wanted to make too much of our good-bye.

"Well, I guess I'll talk to you soon," I said.

"Yeah, e-mail me when you get home."

Sam suddenly perked up. "Hey, what are you doing for your birthday?" she asked, referring to our mutual thirteenth birthday on October 26.

"I hadn't thought about it."

"Maybe my mom and I can fly out to Chicago. Wouldn't that be cool?"

"Totally cool."

"All right, then. Later."

"See ya."

I turned to walk away, but after a few steps Sam's voice turned me back around.

"Hey, Tyler."

"What?"

"Nice jacket."

"Thanks," I said as a big smile spread across my face.

I was wearing my *Kids* jacket the next morning as Pete, in typical fashion, got us to the airport just in time for our flight. He left the car in the white zone, where he would be sure to find a ticket on its windshield when he returned, and escorted us to the gate. Raphael gave Pete a big bear hug, and then my mom and Pete hugged, with my mom getting a little teary as she thanked him for everything he'd done for me, including getting me to the hospital when I'd had my asthma attack. "I'm still mad at you for not telling me the truth about that," she chided.

"Laura, we have to get on the plane," Raphael said, giving her a tug.

The two of them went to board the plane, but I hung back for a moment with Pete.

"Come on, Tyler, we need to get going," Raphael called out. My mom then said something to Raphael that I'm sure had to do with giving Pete and me a moment to say good-bye, because he then said, "We'll see you on board."

"Well, pal, you did all right," Pete said, smiling at me.

"Thanks," I said. "So did you."

"Yeah, I guess I did. It's been a good couple of weeks. Hey, I've got one small piece of advice before you go."

"What?"

"If you like this writing thing at all, pay attention in English. It may seem boring now, but it'll really come in handy later. I wish I'd paid better attention."

"Okay, I will." We stood there for a moment. There was so much I wanted to say but I didn't know where to begin. I finally said, "Thanks for everything, Pete." That small statement didn't seem adequate for what I felt inside but it would have to do.

"My pleasure."

He walked me toward the gate. "Hey, are you dating Kari or not?" I asked.

Pete just grinned. "Let's just wait and see," he said.

We shook hands. I turned around to find the oldest flight attendant in the world waiting to take my ticket.

"How was your trip?" she asked.

"Classic banana peel," I said, smiling. "Classic banana peel."

ABOUT THE AUTHOR

Steve Atinsky has written for the CBS sitcom *Payne* and Disney's *The Weekenders*. *Tyler on Prime Time* is his first novel.

He lives in Santa Monica, California.